It was a danc

The woman stalked her partner—her lucky, lucky partner—with a predatory sexuality. Every move was eloquent, hot and demanding, every glance one of seduction.

Brady stared at Thea's face as the dancers whirled past. Her eyes, wide and lovely, were deep as sin. They were the kind of eyes that could hold a man spellbound. Then she closed them, her lashes black fans on her cheeks as she gave herself over to the pounding, driving music.

The dancers came before them, their steps now slow, now quick, circling one another in a choreographed seduction that had Brady's body tightening with need. The dancers teased, tormented, stepping ever closer to the edge of the crowd.

Then Thea's eyes flicked open and she stared directly at Brady, her gaze filled with desire.

"Would you like to dance with me?"

Blaze™

Dear Reader,

Writing is a journey of discovery. In the case of a group like the Supper Club, there are a lot of characters to know and follow. Most were speaking with their own voices in my head from the beginning (trust me, it gets loud in there sometimes). Thea was so self-contained, so internalized it was hard to really figure out who she was and what she needed. I knew where she'd come from, I knew what had happened to her in New York, but I didn't really know *her*. Discovering her personality and sense of humor, watching her learn about how to live life from a free spirit like Brady McMillan (and a silly pug named Darlene) has been a delight. Meanwhile, the stories of the other characters, particularly Kelly's, continue. Stay tuned for more.

I hope you'll drop me a line at Kristin@kristinhardy.com and let me know what you think. Look for the series to wind up with a bang with Delaney's story in April 2007. To keep track, sign up for my newsletter at www.kristinhardy.com, where you can also find contests, recipes and updates on my recent and upcoming releases.

Have fun,

Kristin Hardy

Books by Kristin Hardy
HARLEQUIN BLAZE

HOT MOVES
Kristin Hardy

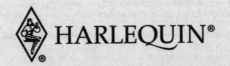

HARLEQUIN®

TORONTO • NEW YORK • LONDON
AMSTERDAM • PARIS • SYDNEY • HAMBURG
STOCKHOLM • ATHENS • TOKYO • MILAN • MADRID
PRAGUE • WARSAW • BUDAPEST • AUCKLAND

ISBN-13: 978-0-373-79311-2
ISBN-10:   0-373-79311-1

HOT MOVES

Copyright © 2007 by Chez Hardy LLC.

To Brian, the check is in the mail
To Kathryn and Teresa, more than usual
And to Stephen, more than you can ever know

Prologue

"I KNEW YOU GUYS WERE up to something." Eyes alight with fun, Thea Mitchell glanced at her friends clustered around the restaurant table. They'd met the year before on the drama department's production of *Henry VI*. The friendships formed had stuck.

"It's your birthday," said Cilla Danforth, wardrobe mistress, leaning out of the way to allow the waiter to take her plate. "Anyway, the costumes are almost done and the dress rehearsal isn't until next week, so no reason we shouldn't sneak out of the workshop early to celebrate."

"The backdrops and props are ready to go," added set designer Paige Favreau, who'd rather predictably gotten her work finished weeks before.

Trish Dawson stirred. "Everyone's got their copies of the final script." And as script doctor, it was her business to know. "If the choreography's set, then we're ready."

"Done last week." Thea stroked her fingers along the magenta feather boa Cilla had given her to wear along with a rhinestone tiara that crowned her thick tumble of dark hair. "I'm on top of my moves."

"So's the guy over at the bar. He's been watching you

all night," said the play's publicity manager Delaney Phillips. The man in question was dark-haired and intense, handsome if you liked the *GQ* type.

Thea didn't, much. "I'll pass. Now him," she added, glancing over at a tousled blonde drinking a beer. "He's definitely my kind of guy." He glanced over and caught her looking and she blushed a little but held his gaze.

"So what's your birthday resolution?" Trish asked, invoking what had become a group ritual.

"Hmm? Oh, I don't know. To have fun."

Delaney imitated a buzzer on a game show. "Too vague, Mitchell. Try again."

Thea grinned. "Okay, how about this? To take more chances." Then her attention was drawn by candles flickering on a cake being carried to her by the waiter. "Like on this chocolate cake for example. I'll take a chance on it any day."

Sabrina Pantolini, from the film department, got up with her camera. Whether she was armed with her camcorder or her Nikon, if Sabrina didn't capture it in pictures, she never quite felt like it had happened. "Okay, everybody lean in and say 'sex,'" she ordered.

"Can't we just have sex, instead?" Thea pouted.

"You can do that, too, birthday girl," Kelly, the group's journalist told her. "Just make a wish and blow out the candles."

Thea winked. "Make a wish? How about me and Blondie?"

"Better blow hard," Delaney suggested.

"I blow just right," Thea told her. She took a breath and turned to the cake.

"Excuse me."

And the breath whooshed out of her lungs as she looked up, snuffing out only part of the candles.

The man from the bar stood over her. He was taller than she'd estimated when he was sitting. Up close, he was clearly older, forties, maybe, with a look of command in his pale eyes. Eyes that focused solely on Thea.

"I see congratulations are in order." His gaze zeroed in on her lips, skimmed the neckline of her low-cut red T-shirt. "What's your name?"

"Thea," she replied.

"Happy birthday, Thea. My name's Derek." Cilla's eyes widened. He didn't notice, nor did Thea. "You've got ten candles on the cake. Is that how old you are, ten?"

"Nineteen," she responded without thinking.

"It could still work," he murmured, almost to himself. "That skin's perfect." He cleared his throat. "Listen, sorry to interrupt your party but I've got something to talk with you about. Alone," he added, glancing over the group clustered around the table, avidly watching them. "Come over to the bar with me."

"Much as I'd like to talk about my perfect skin, I'll pass, thanks." Thea gestured to the cake. "I'm kind of busy right now."

"Trust me, you're not too busy for this. I think you'll be interested in what I have to say."

She eyed him. "If you want to hit on me, here's as good a place as any."

"I'm not hitting on you," he said with a trace of impatience. "This is business, and I don't have all night. Now, you can keep sucking down Shirley Temples with your girl-friends or you can come talk to me about what just might be your future." He tossed a business card down on the table. "I'll be over at the bar."

Turning on his heel, he strode away.

Thea stared at him, watching as he slid onto a stool and gestured for a drink. On the cake before her, a lone candle still sputtered.

"What was that all about?" Trish asked, mystified.

"Ignore him," Paige advised. "He's selling something."

Delaney lifted her club soda. "Nope. Pickup line, no matter what he says."

"No," Cilla and Kelly said simultaneously. "That's Derek Edes," Cilla added.

Sabrina frowned. "I know that name."

"You should. He's only one of the biggest fashion photographers in the business, outside of maybe Richard Avedon."

"Avedon?" Now Thea looked as mystified as Trish. "What does he want with me?"

"Your perfect skin?" Cilla shrugged. "Don't ask me, ask him. He's staring at you again, by the way."

Thea shifted.

"Don't look," Paige ordered. "If he wanted to talk to you badly enough to come over here, he can wait. It's your birthday."

Cilla reached out for the business card, tapping it thoughtfully on the tabletop. "I say wait and call him Monday."

"Or call his room," Kelly added. "I think I read somewhere that he always stays at the Chateau Marmont when he comes to L.A."

Thea rose. "No. I'm going to go find out what he wants."

Delaney snorted. "That's not hard, sweetie. You're gorgeous and he's male."

Thea shook her head. "This isn't sex. It's something else," she said. "I just don't know what."

And so they watched as she crossed the room with a feline grace that was partly the result of fifteen years of dance training, partly innate. They watched as she sat next to him, as he rested a casual, proprietary hand on the back of her stool. They stared as her mouth dropped open in shock, as the five minutes stretched into twenty.

And they watched as she crossed the room, finally, walking as though her feet weren't touching the ground.

"So? What's it all about?" Delaney demanded.

"A job," Thea said, bemused. "He wants me to come to New York and model for a new cosmetics campaign he's shooting."

"What did you say?"

"Remember my birthday resolution?"

"To take more chances?"

She nodded, her eyes on Derek Edes, the blonde completely forgotten. "I said yes. I leave Monday."

1

Portland, Oregon, 2007

"YOU'RE GOING TO SEATTLE for the weekend to drink beer?"

Brady McMillan looked up from the steel keg he was washing out in the pub's microbrewery and grinned at his older brother. "Pour beer, Michael" he corrected, resting a hand against one of the gleaming copper tanks lined up behind him. "It's a brewers' festival. I'll be bonding with the masses, making a good impression for McMillans', comparing notes with my fellow brewmasters—"

"—and drinking beer," Michael finished.

Brady's lips twitched as he lifted the keg to drain onto the concrete floor. Water streamed down to the grates below the funnel-shaped bottoms of the tanks. "It's a difficult job but someone's got to do it. I'm willing to suffer to give McMillans' the best beer possible." Five feet away, on the other side of the low wooden barrier, lay the warm golden oak and leather of their flagship brewpub. Here behind the barrier was Brady's territory of malts and worts, hops and hoses.

Michael folded his arms over his barrel chest. "Some people just use message boards."

"There's no substitute for face-to-face contact."

"Or mouth to glass."

"The taste, the aroma, the mouth feel—"

"The buzz."

"What? I can't hear you over the noise of all the people out in the pub drinking my beer." Brady blinked guilelessly and set the keg upright. "Good thing I go to these festivals to stay on top of the trends."

"Yeah, yeah, yeah. So it's the beer that brings them back, but it's the atmosphere in the pubs that gets 'em here in the first place."

"No doubt. Lucky we're both good at our jobs, isn't it?" Michael was burly where Brady was lanky, darkhaired where Brady was blond, and Michael thrived on the business side of things whereas for Brady it was all about the beer and the people, in roughly that order.

"I think you could start offloading some of your brewing work and pitch in on the pubs some more. Like the Odeon Theater property. We need to go over some of the numbers. The deal's supposed to close week after next and we've got to talk about the closing costs and go over some construction figures—"

"Oh, hey, look, the beer needs me," Brady said quickly, lips twitching. "Wow. Bad timing. Wish I could help."

Michael's brows lowered. "You're not making beer, you're washing kegs."

"Sterilizing," Brady corrected.

"Whatever. This whole theater thing was your idea. You can at least pretend to be interested in the remodel."

"I'm the beer guy and the idea man, remember? You're the pub guy."

"I'm willing to share the pub guy part."

"Hah." Brady held out his hand, pointing to a thin white scar on the side of his forefinger. "See that?"

"What?"

"That's from the time you attacked me with your letter opener when I tried to open up QuickBooks."

Michael took a closer look and snorted. "You got that playing mumblety-peg with Elliot Bingenheimer in third grade."

"Oh, you can tell yourself that if it makes you feel better." Brady flexed his hand meditatively. "They tell me I'll be able to play Parcheesi again someday."

"Yeah, that's why you went rock climbing last week."

"It's physical therapy. Face it, Michael, you're a control freak. You say you want to share your pub guy thing but you know you don't."

"Unlike you, say, who's happy to delegate…oh, gee, that's right, nothing," he said lightly. "You know, you might be able to keep up brewing at four pubs, but when we add the new place, even you're going to have to let go of some things. At least if you want to keep up with your kayaking and mountain biking schedule. We should hire a brewmaster for each place."

"My name's on it," Brady said stubbornly. "I want to be sure it's my beer."

"Now who's the control freak?"

Humor glimmered in Brady's eyes. "All right." He set the keg aside. "Even though I *am* just the beer and idea guy, let's talk about your theater."

"My theater? *My* theater, Mr. 'This Is A One Of A Kind Property And We Have To Buy It Now'? *Our* theater," Michael corrected. "Or it will be."

Brady wiped off his hands and settled his ball cap more firmly on his head. "Yep. That it will."

SOME BIRTHDAYS WERE rites of passage, Thea thought as she washed her hands in the blue glass basin in the bathroom of the L.A. restaurant. She discarded the drying napkin then stopped, staring at herself in the mirror. She wasn't given to primping—she habitually skinned her hair back in a ponytail or braid, rarely bothered with cosmetics. With clever makeup and the right hairstyle, her full mouth and wideset eyes could take on a singular beauty—or so said the fashion editors and designers who'd paid a thousand dollars an hour for her time during the three years she'd modeled. Without the hair and makeup, Thea thought her features just looked overstated to the point of caricature on her angular face.

The bee-stung lips and soft gray-blue eyes came from her mother. The angular facial structure and sharp jaw came from her father, though his was always tight with bitterness or poised to deliver some cutting comment. She'd have preferred to look at herself and see nothing of either of them, but they were part of her physical makeup. Ingrained in her emotional makeup, too, no matter how hard she might battle to erase them.

No, she wasn't given to primping anymore. So why was she standing here now, looking at herself, searching for a remnant of the excited young girl she'd been all those birthdays before? At twelve, bursting with anticipation in the days before the birthday that would make her a teenager. At seventeen, sitting on the cusp of adulthood, desperate to move out and escape her overbearing father.

The next significant milestone, twenty-one, didn't bear thinking about, lost at a time she'd lost herself. And she couldn't really say she'd ever found herself again in the fog of time that had passed since.

With an impatient noise, she turned for the door.

There was a cake on the table when she got back to it, glimmering with candles. Nine more of them than at the last milestone. Nine years... And where had they left her now?

Sabrina glanced up with laughter in her dark eyes. "About time you got back. We thought you'd drowned."

"It was a near thing, but I made it to shore."

"You should have yelled if you were in trouble," Kelly said. "We could have sent in our sexy waiter to rescue you."

"Hey, expectant mothers and soon-to-be brides aren't supposed to notice other guys," Trish reminded her.

"Other guys who aren't their intended," Paige clarified, pushing a smooth wing of blond hair behind one ear.

"Exactly."

"I was only being descriptive," Kelly said with dignity, taking a drink of the mango juice she'd ordered. "We writers do that."

"'Zat so?" Thea sat down and pulled in her chair.

"Well, you've got to admit, he is sexy. I suppose I could have said hot. That's a synonym. We writers use those, too."

"Glad you clarified that for me." Thea glanced at the waiter across the room. She'd spent so long consciously shutting off that line of thought, not thinking about men, how they looked, how they acted, whether she might want them in her life.

Whether they might want her.

The waiter glanced over and their gazes met for a moment, the quick connection like the flash of light from the revolving lantern of a lighthouse. Such a circumscribed life she led, so few people she touched—the Supper Club and the acquaintances she'd made at tango class—so few people she even made eye contact with. She'd forgotten what it was like.

"Time for wishes and resolutions," Trish announced.

"And cake," Delaney added.

"Hurry up. I'm suffering a chocolate deficiency," Kelly said. "It can't be good for the baby."

"Don't rush her," Trish scolded. "Take your time, Thea."

"I'll have to. I've got to come up with something pretty good to keep up with what all the rest of you guys have done this year."

"You don't have to worry about keeping up."

Thea grinned. "I couldn't if I wanted to." Not with this group of friends: Trish, who'd made her dream of being a Hollywood screenwriter a reality; Cilla, now a sought-after clothing designer and retail entrepreneur; Sabrina, who'd turned her fascination with cameras into a documentary filmmaking career; Kelly, a top reporter at the biggest film industry daily. Even Paige and Delaney had done well, if less publicly, Paige with her own interior design business and Delaney moving up at her marketing firm.

Only Thea was no further along with her life than she'd been when they'd met at eighteen, save for the robust investment accounts that were her only tangible souvenirs of her time in New York.

It was definitely enough to make a person think.

"So what's your birthday resolution?" Cilla asked. "No cake until you tell us."

"To get my life in gear." The words were out before Thea knew she was going to say them.

And she swore everyone at the table stilled for an instant.

"Well, how about that?" Sabrina said finally. "You don't take on the small stuff, do you?"

"So what does getting your life in gear mean?" That was Paige—figure out your goal and set about accomplishing it.

"I don't know," Thea confessed. "I just want something…different."

The table erupted in conversation. "Different is great." Cilla stared at her with a broad grin. Had it been that obvious that she'd been going through the motions, Thea wondered.

"You could go back to school, finish your degree," Trish suggested.

"Do you want to get into film?" Sabrina asked. "I have an opening for a production assistant."

Paige nodded. "Or you could start your own business."

"Why would she need the headaches?" Delaney took a sip of her Cosmopolitan. "She's got all the money she could want socked away in the bank. You ask me, she should only do what she wants to do."

"And what is that?" Sabrina asked.

If she only knew, Thea thought. "Right now, it's having cake." For the rest, she had time. She leaned in to blow out the candles.

"Don't forget to make your wish," Kelly reminded her.

Just to be happy, finally. It was time, Thea thought, looking around the table of glowing faces. Things had changed for her friends in more than the career department. All of them were in love. All of them, save unrepentantly single Delaney, had found their soul mates.

Not that Thea was looking for that. When it came to men, she didn't trust her judgment a lick. She didn't trust the whole breed, for that matter, though her Supper Club friends seemed happy with their husbands and lovers so far. She needed to take it slowly, start with getting her life rolling again.

She took a breath and blew.

THEA AND TRISH STOOD at the valet stand, the last two waiting for their cars.

"So how are things?" Thea asked her. "You look happy."

"I am." A smile bloomed across her face, slow and beautiful. "I never realized I could be, not like this. I know that sounds goofy but it's true. I keep thinking it's all a dream and I'm going to wake up but I think it's real."

Thea admired her, the luminous skin that glowed against the red hair, the loveliness that Trish had hidden for so long. Until she'd met Ty. "It doesn't sound goofy. It sounds nice."

"I wish I could bottle it and give some to everyone I know." Trish paused. "I wish I could give some to you."

"I'm all right," Thea said.

"Are you?"

"Better every day."

Trish looked at her and nodded. "I almost believe that. You seem different tonight. I don't know how, but different."

"Spring fever."

"Not spring anymore," Trish corrected. "We're in June. New season, new life."

"We'll see." The valet drove up with Trish's car, a sporty convertible. She traded tip for key and leaned in to hug Thea. "Happy birthday, sweetie. Here's hoping this is your year."

"My year for what?"

"For getting it all."

She got in and drove away with a wave, while Thea watched. *Here's hoping this is your year.*

Thea's cell phone rang as the valet pulled up with her Prius. She flipped open the handset. "Hello?"

"I need your moves," said the person on the other end.

Thea blinked. "Excuse me?"

"I need you, now."

"Is this an obscene phone call?" she demanded.

"You wish," answered a voice she recognized.

Thea handed the valet his tip. "You're a sick woman, Waller."

Robyn Waller, one of the few true friends Thea had made in New York. They'd met in a dance class Thea had taken to keep sharp. Since then Thea's dance dreams had been channeled into amateur ballroom dancing and Robyn's had been rescaled to owning a dance studio in her Portland, Oregon, hometown.

"So what's going on? Why do you need my moves? Assuming I feel like giving any of them away, of course." Tucking her tongue into her cheek, Thea got into her car and buckled on her seatbelt.

"Well, are you still working one of your McJobs, or do you actually have something you care about?"

When your retirement was already in the bank, earning enough for most of your income besides, a career became optional. "I'm working at a nursery."

"Babies?"

Thea laughed. "Plants. Why, you want to come down for a visit?"

"Just the opposite. What would you say to coming up to Portland for a couple of months, teach in my studio?"

Thea snorted and pulled out into traffic. "I'd say it's a long commute for a temp job."

"I'm serious, Thea. I need you, if you can do it."

There was something in Robyn's voice, she realized. An urgency, an anxiety. "Robyn, I'm not qualified to teach," she protested.

"Oh, come on, you know top level figures for all the Latin and smooth styles and you're the best amateur Argentine tango dancer I know."

"For the women's parts, not the men's. I'd need that to teach."

"You can learn."

"What happened? Why the panic?"

Robyn blew out an impatient breath. "My lead instructor's husband got transferred to Chicago. She's leaving in a week. I just found out today."

"Ouch. There have got to be more qualified people up your way, though."

"If there are, I haven't had any luck finding them. And there's a little thing called my vacation."

Thea's eyes widened. "Oh no! Australia."

"Yeah, Australia. Everything's already paid for. Three weeks Down Under. My cousin and I have been planning this for a year."

"Three *weeks*?"

"Three and a half, actually. It costs so much to get there and it takes so long, it hardly makes sense otherwise. Plus, there's so much to see."

"Yeah, but wow, the timing's bad."

"Tell me about it."

Thea slipped into the left turn lane. "Can't your instructor stay a bit longer?"

"She's got a two-year-old and a four-year-old. They've all got to move at the same time and that's got to be soon."

"I guess that's a 'no.'"

"That's a no," Robyn agreed.

"And you can't find anyone?"

"No one I want to leave with my business, lock, stock and barrel immediately after they start, anyway."

Thea turned with the yellow light, zipping across just ahead of a speeding Nissan Maxima. "I guess I can kind of see your point."

"I leave next Friday. If you can get up here in a day or two, we'd have time to get you up to speed. You can stay at my place. Darlene will keep you company while I'm gone." Darlene, Robyn's irrepressible pug. She and Thea had become fast friends on earlier visits.

"You'll have my car to get around." Robyn paused. "Thea, I really need you. I know it's a lot to ask, but will you do it?"

To get my life in gear. A chance to get out of L.A., a chance to teach dance instead of potting plants for a living. A chance to help Robyn out at a crucial time, Robyn, who'd been there for her once, long ago. A chance for…who knew?

"I won't need your car. I'll drive up," Thea said.

"You'll drive up?" Robyn stopped. "Does that mean…"

"Give me two days so I can stop and see my sister in Sacramento. I'll be up Thursday."

"That gives us almost a week. That's perfect. You're perfect."

"Well, I'm glad you've finally realized that," Thea said.

2

"WHY DO I FEEL LIKE I should have a hall pass?" Thea asked Robyn as they walked down the broad hallway of the Lincoln School. Eighteen years had passed since she'd graduated from sixth grade, but the black-and-white-tiled floor and the glassed-in display cases on the walls brought it all back. All she needed was the beaded metal chain from her I.D. tag to use as her hopscotch marker and she'd be set.

"Just wait," Robyn said.

"Tell me you're not going to take me to the principal's office."

"Nope. Someplace better." She stopped before a wooden door with Cafeteria emblazoned on its frosted glass insert.

"Let me guess. You're taking me out for sloppy joes?"

"If you're good," Robyn promised and swung the door open.

It reminded her of her elementary school cafeteria, only homier, friendlier. Butter yellow walls, black-and-white tile and polished chrome, in a room buzzing with conversation and laughter. Straight ahead lay the counter with its row of stools. Waitresses in thirties-style diner uniforms circulated with laden trays. Behind the counter lay not only the window to the kitchen but a full bar with a dizzying array of taps; on the far wall, copper-clad brewing tanks gleamed.

Thea turned around with a broad grin. "This is the coolest place I've ever seen."

Robyn laughed. "I knew you'd love it. Wait until you see the bathrooms. It's just like you remember from being a kid, only better."

They threaded their way to a table that overlooked a playground mostly occupied by the staked green rows of a kitchen garden, but still boasting a swing set and slide off to one side, and yes, a hopscotch grid on which a trio of animated girls hotly contested the lead.

"They grow a lot of their own vegetables right here," Robyn explained, taking the menu the hostess handed her. "About the best salads you'll get in town, even at the farmers' market. Although you can also get a sloppy joe."

Thea shook her head. "It's brilliant."

"It's the McMillans. Brilliance is their specialty."

"A chain?"

"Brothers," Robyn explained. "They've got a string of places. Some of them are just brewpubs, some are pub hotels, or even spas. But they pick up these quirky themes— one of the places is a decommissioned jail, and they converted the old county work farm. Oh, and then there's Suds n' Celluloid. It shows old movies. You kick back on sofas and old chairs and waiters bring you beer and food."

"Now, that's what I call civilization," Thea commented. "They'd clean up in L.A."

Robyn grinned. "Sorry, they're pretty much a Portland-only gig. When everything you touch turns to gold, you don't have to go far. I should be so lucky," she trailed off.

"Business tough?" Thea asked sympathetically, after they'd ordered.

Robyn moved her water glass around. "It's going well,

just not fast enough. It's always hard the first couple of years, I knew that getting into it. I'm hanging in there." She squared her shoulders and rearranged the cutlery.

"You know, if you needed a loan—" Thea began.

"Yeah, I know," Robyn said and gave her hand a brief squeeze. "I don't want to go there, though. I'm already asking enough of you by hauling you up here on zero notice. You walked away from your job."

"My McJob," Thea pointed out. "I'll find a new one."

"Even so."

"Robyn, you were there for me, remember? There's no way I can ever pay you back for that."

"That's what friends do."

"Exactly," Thea said. "You have to go. You've been talking about going to Australia someday for as long as I've known you. Besides, you need time to yourself, time to recharge. Just think, in a week you'll be flying off to do just that."

"What about you? When do you recharge?"

Thea grinned as the waitress brought their beer. "Shoot, I've spent the last eight years recharging. I'm powered up, now."

"Yeah, I buy that." Robyn raised her glass. "To being powered up."

"To being powered up," Thea echoed, and the ring of their toast echoed out. A moment later, Thea blinked. "Wow, that is some seriously wonderful beer," she said. "Maybe that's what you need to do, set up a microbrewery in your dance studio. Robyn's Tango Ale. Just like the McMillans."

"Honey, there's nobody like the McMillans. They're a force unto themselves."

BRADY AND MICHAEL STOOD on the threadbare carpeting and looked around the Odeon Theater. The seats had been upholstered in plush red velvet some seventy-odd years before. Now the worn fabric was faded to a rusty dun color, mottled with stains. Overhead arched a trompe l'oeil ceiling, bordered by gold-leafed carvings. The stale air smelled faintly of cigarette smoke.

Michael scanned the rows. "Don't really want to think about what's on those seats."

"Given that the last movie they showed here was *Horny Coeds Going Wild,* that's probably smart."

"They all come out, first thing," Michael decided.

"Probably smart, too."

"It's a great space. The question is, how do we turn this into a brewpub?"

Brady began to amble down the aisle. "Same way we did with the jail and the Lincoln School. Think outside the box. The two floors above here will be the hotel. This is the common area. We add a bar at the back, take out a lot of the seats and put in tables. Leave in the box seats."

"And what, show movies here, too?" Michael followed Brady to the stage.

"Naw. We're already doing that at Suds n' Celluloid. We need to do something else with this."

"Such as what, idea man?"

Brady boosted himself up onto the chest-high wood platform. "I dunno." He stood staring around, hands in his pockets. "We'll figure it out."

"It'd be nice to figure it out before we pop a couple million buying and renovating it," Michael said dryly.

"Yep." He could see it, Brady thought, even through the shabbiness. It had been built in the heyday of the thirties movie palaces, with the sweeping curves of gilded wood, the opulent carvings, the private boxes that rose along the walls. High overhead soared the crenellated wood arch that framed the stage. Heavy gold velvet curtains, now falling apart under their own weight, hid the wings. He could see it cleaned and painted and polished, hear the laughter and the buzz of conversation as the tables of diners held their beers and looked up at…

What?

"We'll figure it out," he said again.

At the sound of a throat clearing, they both looked up to see the seller's agent standing at the top of one of the aisles. "Have you gentlemen seen everything you wanted to see?" she asked, making a show of checking her watch. She had better things to do at eight o'clock on a Friday night than show real estate, her posture clearly telegraphed.

Brady and Michael glanced at each other and nodded. "Yeah, I think so," Michael said. They started back up the aisle.

Outside, the air was warm in the last light of a summer evening. "Where are you parked?" Brady asked.

"By the Cascade Brewery," Michael said, naming their flagship brewpub on the other side of the downtown.

"Me too." They ambled along to turn onto Front Street. "We've got a great entry area," Brady said. "Classic old-time theater. We keep that the same. Maybe have someone in the ticket booth to take people's names."

"Stuck out there in the middle of that coved entry area? Is that going to be practical?"

Brady shrugged. "We find a way to make it practical. It's like the Lincoln School, we keep as much of the vibe as we can. Make up sheets that look like movie posters advertising the specials and seasonal beers, mix 'em in with pulp movie posters, sheets pushing whatever the entertainment is."

"Yeah, whatever the entertainment is," Michael echoed with a sidelong glance at him.

"You can't push creative brilliance," Brady said mildly.

Michael laughed. "I'll remember that. Lindsay keeps telling me we're nuts."

"The woman's going to be giving birth to your kid for the third time—"

"Kids," Michael interjected. "Twins, remember?"

"Kids. And she says *we're* nuts?"

"She says the hormones make her forget what labor's like."

Brady snorted. "It'd take a lot more than hormones for me."

"You're right about the property, though, it is a great property. Not that it shouldn't be, for that price."

"Hell, we convert the levels above the hotel floors to lofts and offices, we can probably make most of the mortgage off the rents."

"Possibly."

Brady shook his head pityingly. "You're a pessimist, Michael."

"And you're way too much of an optimist."

"One of my many fine qualities."

"It'll cost to renovate the office space, too, you know," Michael reminded him. "We won't get to it right away and there's no way we'll rent them all."

"That's okay. We'll start small, give the place a chance to get hip, generate some buzz." Brady grinned. "We can put signs up by the bar, 'If you lived here, you'd be home now.' Hell, I'd live there."

"You'd live anywhere that was close to your beer."

"You know, that's not a bad idea. I could read it bedtime stories before I went to sleep."

"There's something twisted about you," Michael muttered.

Ahead of them, the broad swath of the Willamette River bisected the city on its way to join with the Columbia. The lights of the Hawthorne Bridge glimmered in the fading light. On the broad sweep of the waterfront park that paralleled the riverbank, a crowd of people were gathered. Music floated across on the night air.

"Oh, gee, let me guess," Michael said, "another festival."

"The joys of culture. Maybe we'll be lucky and find out it's a beer festival." Brady hooked his hands in his back pockets.

"You really are an optimist."

"They'll have food, anyway. I'm starved."

"You just ate dinner two hours ago."

"Exactly. Time enough to get hungry again."

It wasn't about eating, though, he saw as they crossed the street to skirt the edge of the park. It was about the sound, the motion.

It was about the dance.

Moonlight and Tango read a banner. Curious, Brady wandered closer.

"Thinking about auditioning for 'Dancing with the Stars'?" Michael asked.

Brady grinned. "Never know. I might need a backup if the theater doesn't work out."

Piano and strings, the slow, insistent thud of percussion. The exotic rhythms of the music whispered of passion, of dim, intimate cafés where couples embraced in the dance. Paper lanterns dangled from the trees. Ahead, people clustered around a spot in the open, watching. And beyond them, he glimpsed motion, color—a couple, dancing.

Something about the music intrigued him. Something about it had him wanting to see more.

"We don't have all night," Michael reminded him.

"Relax, will you? You can head out, I've got my truck. I want to see this." He ignored Michael's grumbling and moved closer. And when he got near enough to look past them, he saw.

She wore red, a narrow dress slit all the way up the thigh on one side to reveal a long, sleek leg jackknifed up to the hip of her partner. A matching red blossom was tucked into the dark hair gathered at the nape of her neck; her back, her arms were naked.

Brady swore that his heart stopped, or maybe it was just the music. When she moved again, with an almost catlike grace, he gulped oxygen out of self-preservation with the same rush of adrenaline he felt when shooting the rapids in his kayak.

He stared at her as the pair moved through their intricately choreographed…seduction. It wasn't one of those artsy dances with all the feathers and floaty dresses. Dark and driven, it was a dance of lust, pure and simple. The woman prowled around her partner—her lucky, lucky partner—with a sort of predatory sexuality, every line of her body, every movement eloquent of heat and demand, every glance one of temptation.

Brady didn't know how but he wanted—no needed— to be near her, touching her, tasting her, discovering the scent of that smooth neck, the taste of that full mouth that looked like some kind of ripe, exotic fruit. He stared at her face, her eyes as the pair whirled past. Wide and lovely, they drew him in, mesmerized him. Then she closed them as she abandoned herself to the dance.

The dancers spun, their steps now slow, now quick, circling around one another. They intertwined their legs in a stylized sequence that was the next best thing to foreplay. Unable to look away, Brady stared, his body tight with need. She was pressed to her partner, a teasing half smile on her face as they stepped ever closer to the edge of the crowd. Her eyes flicked open and she stared directly into Brady's.

And this time, his heart really did stop.

IT WAS WHEN SHE DANCED the tango that Thea felt truly free. She'd draw the silk of one of her dresses over her skin and it would begin, the throb of arousal, the choreography of need. And when the dance began, nothing else mattered. She existed only for the rhythm, for the steps, her body flowing into the movements that became merely extensions of the music.

If the waltz was about romance, tango was about passion, the dance of lovers. For so long she'd existed without any touch but a quick hug from friends and family—and the contact of the dance. Torso to torso, thigh to thigh, the tango somehow refilled the dry well of her soul, renewing her week after week, allowing her to go on.

The night was warm, the stars just beginning to emerge. The seduction of the music eddied through her system. Eyes closed, she concentrated only on the steps and lead of her partner, the light touch of arm, the firm press of hands. She let the dance take control and in doing so became something more than she was, a woman who could trust without fear, feel without consequences.

She felt the stir of longing. Not for her partner, Paul— a myopic shoe salesman with a wife and three kids—but for the touch of a man, the feel of a body against hers for the sake of her, not for the sake of a dance.

Paul pulled her to a stop near the crowd. Thea flicked her leg around his in a *gancho,* snapping her head to the side to stare at the people.

And heat punched through her. She swayed, lips parting in shock. And she stared, stunned, even when the dance whirled her away.

He stood at the fringe, part of the crowd, but separate. His gaze fixed on hers with a naked wanting that snatched the breath from her lungs. In the dim light, she couldn't see the color of his eyes. It didn't matter: blue or brown, gray or green, she could see, feel, sense the desire. He stood a distance away but she could have been in his arms. Suddenly all the unfocused need she felt, all the passion she'd always invested in the dance, coalesced. Paul's touch became the feel of this unknown stranger.

Paul spun her back into the center of the circle. She obeyed his lead, swiveling left and right before him teasingly, though it was the stranger she moved for. She and Paul stalked each other in the ritualized pursuit of the dance but it was the stranger she wanted. It was the stranger whose touch she craved.

And he never stopped watching her. In the final throes of the routine, she was conscious, always conscious of his gaze and of the arousal that flared within her.

She hardly noticed the end of the song, only that she and Paul were bowing to the crowd amid the surge of applause.

Thea knew what she was to do next. This was a *milonga* designed to recruit more tango enthusiasts for the Portland Tango Club. The showcase was to get them excited about the possibilities; the subsequent impromptu lessons for the onlookers were meant to show them that they could do it, too.

The stranger didn't look like the type who'd be interested in tango. Tall and rangy in jeans and a black T-shirt, he looked more like a guy who spent his time outdoors, hiking, mountain biking, skiing.

Anyway, she was being ridiculous. It was a glance across a dance floor, nothing more. It was the kind of thing people—guys—did all the time, she reminded herself. He probably hadn't even thought twice about it. The only reason it spoke to her was that she didn't have anything even remotely resembling a personal life.

Pathetic, she thought, glancing toward the river. Besides, it wasn't as if she was looking to get caught up with a guy. She was only here for a short job. The strange interlude was best forgotten. She swallowed and turned to where he'd been standing.

Only to find him directly behind her.

"Nice dance."

His eyes were green, she saw in the fading light, deepset, a little sleepy-eyed. His wasn't a conventionally handsome face. The features were too strong: an aggressive nose, sharp cheekbones pushing out against the skin of his angular face. Humor lingered around the corners of his mouth, though, humor and promise from lips that looked way too intriguing. Her heart pumped faster in her chest.

"I'm glad you enjoyed it. You like tango?"

"I'm getting a new appreciation for it by the minute," he

said, giving her a look that had her cheeks warming. "You two were something. Have you been dancing together long?"

"Oh, about four hours." At his surprised expression, she laughed. "I'm visiting. This was a last-minute thing we threw together."

"Don't even try to tell me that you just learned tango today."

Thea nibbled her lip. "Would you buy it?"

His glance sharpened with some special attention. "Right now, I'd buy about anything you tried to sell me," he said. "I'm Brady, by the way."

"I'm Thea. And the answer is no. I've been dancing for about eight years."

"You've been using the time well."

This time, she definitely blushed—she knew it because she saw his grin.

Up front, Robyn turned on the microphone. "Thea, Paul, thanks for that showcase. We're going to go through another figure before the free dance, so if you're interested in learning some tango instead of watching, pair up with a partner and let's get started."

Brady's eyes glimmered. "I guess now's my chance to get you to show me some of those hot moves."

Thea eyed him. "Why do I think you already know all the hot moves you need. Or is it the smooth moves?"

He laughed loudly. "Oh, now that was harsh. For that, you have to teach me." He stepped toward her and raised his hands.

He worked for a living, she thought, staring at them. They were long-fingered, strong, his forearms sinewy and tanned. And she suddenly found herself wondering what it would be like to dance with him, to have those hands on her, to be pressed against his body so tightly that not even air came between them. Why not, she thought suddenly. She was supposed to draw new students. Why shouldn't she touch him, feel him, let him touch her? See what he was made of.

Besides, it was only part of the dance.

"All right, everyone," Robyn was saying. "Line up in pairs, ladies facing me, gentlemen with your backs to me." She walked them through the steps, first the gentlemen, then the ladies. It gave Thea the opportunity to study her new partner.

Lean, balanced, Brady moved with a deceptively careless grace. He didn't seem to be focused on Robyn's direction but he caught on to the steps immediately. And when Thea began moving through the ladies' sequence, he stood, hands on his hips, watching her. "You don't need to stare," she said once as the step took her past him.

"I'm paying attention. I figure I might learn a thing or two." His tone was light, but the heat in his eyes sent something skittering around in her stomach.

"Okay," Robyn said. "Now that we know the basic step, let's get into dance position and try it out. Stand opposite your partners. Ladies, put your left hand on the gentleman's shoulder."

He stepped closer. "Now, about that paying attention," he murmured and Thea's pulse bumped and sped up.

He was tall, she realized. She stood nearly six foot in her bare feet and had grown accustomed to towering over men, especially in high-heeled dance shoes. With Brady, she found herself looking up.

Taking a breath, she put her hand on his shoulder. And swallowed. It didn't matter that she was only touching the cotton of his shirt. Somehow, all she was conscious of was the feel of the hard rise of muscle beneath.

"Gentlemen, put your right hand on the lady's shoulder blade."

His gaze fixed on hers, Brady pressed his hand in place and it was all she could do not to gasp.

He flashed a wicked smile. "Sorry, is my hand cold?"

It wasn't cold at all, and he damned well knew it. Heat spread out from the extravagance of the fingers spread on her bare skin. It felt startlingly intimate. They were in public, among a throng of people. So how was it that she could only think of darkened bedrooms, of how it would feel to have that hand slide over her bare body?

Snap out of it, she told herself.

"Now join your other hands and space yourselves about six to eight inches apart. As you've seen, Argentine tango tends to be danced in a tight, closed position, with the inner thighs of the lady and gentleman pressed together. Those of you who like, step closer."

Eyes staring unwaveringly into hers, Brady moved against her. "I like," he murmured, close enough that she could feel the breath of his words. His fingers tightened slightly on her back, bringing her closer. "Yeah, I like a lot."

Her heart hammered madly in her chest. He was too close, too hot, too *there*. "Easy, big fella," she said as evenly as she could muster. "It's just a dance."

Yet his touch overtook her focus. She needed to concentrate on something safe, Thea thought in a panic. Not those eyes, not those green, green eyes with their glint of humor, not those eyes that made her want. And if she didn't look there, she'd find her gaze slipping down to his mouth, which was way too near. Every time she looked there she found herself wondering what it would feel like to brush her lips against his, wondering how he'd taste. Wondering what he'd do if she leaned in out of the blue and pressed her mouth to his.

Ridiculous, she thought impatiently. The man was a stranger, they were at a *milonga*. It was absurd.

And she couldn't stop wanting it.

So she focused on the point of his jaw. Nice. Safe. Square and strong, darkened a little with a day's growth of beard. If she leaned in and put her face against it, it would be rough, warm. And it would put her closer to that clean scent that didn't seem to have a thing to do with conventional colognes. Maybe shampoo or soap? Whatever it was, if she could get a deep, deep breath of it she thought maybe she could die happy.

The music caught her by surprise when it began. She found him looking down at her in amusement. "You okay?"

"Fine."

He leaned in. "Better focus," he said softly in her ear. "Teachers can't get distracted."

With every step, she could feel his torso shift, as though beneath his clothes his body were stripped down to muscle and sinew and bone. With every step, she became only more aware of him against her. And it sent her mind vaulting along carnal pathways, speculating if this was what it would be like to have him pressed against her naked, on top of her, so that she could feel his every movement as he poised himself over her, bringing all that heat and want and tension and lust—

"Okay, ready for me?"

She stared at him. "What?"

"My hot move."

She gave an uneven laugh. "Sure."

Looking down a bit, he led her through the eight-count

basic that Robyn had taught them. Thea watched his face. He was concentrating on his feet, his lead, working his way through each segment of the figure. His lashes were darker than she'd expected, a sheaf of his hair hanging down over his forehead. "And, done." His eyes flicked up to meet hers.

She felt the jolt all the way to her toes.

"Good memory," she managed, unable to look away.

"You think I'm good at the eight-count basic, just give me a try on something else."

Thea had a pretty good idea he wasn't talking about tango anymore. She stared up at him, watched desire replace the humor, desire overtake everything. He bent his head toward her—

And the song ended.

For a moment neither of them moved, caught in a frozen tableau of awareness, lips a hairsbreadth apart.

Thea moistened her lips. "I should…dance with some-one else now."

"Do you want to?" he asked, not looking away as a new song started.

"It's not a question of want…"

"Then don't. Stay with me." And he pulled her back into his arms.

NIGHT HAD TRULY FALLEN now, the moon high overhead. They danced in the dappled shade of the trees. She was ex-traordinary, Brady thought, looking down at her as they moved through the steps. Shadows pooled dark in the hollow of her collarbone, her shoulder itself milk pale in the moon-light. Beneath his fingertips, her skin was bewitchingly soft. If he stretched more he could press his lips against it, inhale that subtle scent of hers, something that wrapped around his senses and evoked images of candlelit Buenos Aires cafés with slow moving fans turning up by the ceiling.

He could feel his pulse beating the slow thud of demand, like some clock measuring off the moments until they could be together, alone. He thought of the look in her eyes when the first song had ended, a heady mix of arousal, want and seductive surrender. He wanted, needed to see it again—when she was under him, taut and twisting with desire.

The music died away and a new song began. The *milonga* was quieting now, couples spreading out. They'd danced their way to the edge of the area, he saw. "Want to take a break?" he asked.

Thea glanced at the couples. As far as Brady could tell, they seemed to be doing fine. "Maybe for a few minutes."

The two of them walked slowly toward the river walk. Behind them, the music continued. On the pavement, away from the lights, things were quieter, more peaceful. Across the Willamette, lights glimmered, making reflections on the dark water.

"It's so beautiful," Thea murmured. "Most places, they'd cram office buildings and condos and hotels along here."

"Used to be a freeway, then they shut it down and turned it into a park."

"Bravo. Usually it's the other way."

His teeth gleamed in the half-light. "That's Portland. Hell of a town."

"Are you from here?"

"Born and raised. I guess that makes me biased."

"Maybe just a little."

"So how about you? You said you're visiting?"

"My friend Robyn is part of the tango club. She needed a hand…"

"So she brought in a pair of hired stilettos."

He made her laugh. "I guess so. She knows I'm hooked on the dance."

"It shows. You can't dance the way you do without feeling something for it."

"You do it long enough, it becomes a part of you." Thea drifted to a stop and leaned against the railing overlooking the water. "I guess that sounds silly."

"No, it doesn't."

She turned away from the river, looking back at the *milonga*. A breeze stirred the lanterns in the trees. Their moving patterns of light and shadow silhouetted the figures dancing. A woman's voice, throaty with longing, floated through the evening air; and behind it, the instruments formed a mournful chorus.

"She sounds heartbroken," Brady murmured. He stepped away from the railing, slipping one hand along to cover Thea's, swinging around to come slowly to a stop before her.

"She is. *'Mi Noche Triste.'* My sad night," she translated. "It's a very famous song in tango."

"Do you know the story?" He leaned in to press his hands on the rails, trapping her between them, his gaze holding her transfixed.

"She weeps for a lover who has abandoned her. She sits in the dark. At night, she falls asleep with the door ajar because it lets her imagine that he is coming home. That's tango, the dance of longing."

"What do you long for?"

"What makes you think I long for anything?" He was close to her now, so close.

"Everybody wants something." His lips were a fraction away from hers.

"And you? What do you want?"

"That's easy." He could tell she felt his breath as he said the words. "I want you."

And then he leaned in and took.

3

IT WAS A BIG, WIDE WORLD, but somehow the entire thing reduced down to just one sensation—the press of Brady's lips to hers. Thea stood absolutely still, not even breathing, every fiber of her attuned to it. Mesmerizing warmth, a surprising softness, a beguiling friction that tempted her lips to part.

Her breath shuddered out.

And then, oh, then, the taste of him, the slick dance of tongues that sent butterflies flitting about her stomach and a slow roll of tension forming within her.

She felt herself trembling. Everything in her clamored to dive into the kiss hard and deep, to crush him against her, but here he'd barely touched her and she was quivering. And it rocked her in some fundamental way. She wasn't a virgin, but there was some part of her that wasn't really touched, some part of her that would be his alone.

And so Thea kissed him.

She'd wondered as the years rolled by what it might be like. She'd wondered if she'd forgotten how, if she'd be able to relax and enjoy it any more. But with his mouth on hers, she let all that go and immersed herself in the kiss. Her hands framed his face, fingers threaded through his hair. Changing the angle of the kiss, she nipped at his lips, her tongue dancing against his. Her soft exhale was a barely audible moan.

And suddenly everything changed. She'd kissed men during her life, even once or twice in the years since New York, but it had never been like this, this overwhelming surge of sensation. She'd kissed men but it had never raked her with wanton need. She didn't want easy exploration any more. She wanted it relentless and direct. In a flash, she turned the kiss hard, lacing it with demand.

Brady's hands clenched the railings until his knuckles whitened.

Thea trailed kisses along his jaw, making an impatient noise down in her throat. She traced her fingers down his chest, nuzzled against him.

She could feel him getting hard.

"Don't you want to touch me?" she breathed, her hands lingering around his belt, slipping under his untucked T-shirt to trace the lines of his abs.

He gave in and crushed her to him.

She hoped her low laugh told him she didn't want gentle any more—she wanted it as hard and fast and urgent as he did.

He ran his fingers up the length of her thigh and into the high, high slit of her dress. And when she raised her leg up farther and wrapped it around his waist, it about snatched her breath away. So close, yet not close enough. All she wanted was to feel him naked against her.

"I think we need to get somewhere private," Brady said raggedly.

"Now," was all she said, urgency throbbed in her voice.

"My truck's close. We can go to my place," he added. "It'll be quick."

"I hope so," she said.

The trip to the truck took too long, or maybe it only seemed that way because he kept stopping and pressing her body up against a lamppost or a building so that he could fuse his mouth to hers, kissing her like he was storing up oxygen enough for the next part of the journey.

She didn't want to wait, Thea thought as Brady helped her into the Jeep. She needed him now. Needed more now. She shifted when he got in, pressing a hot, open-mouthed kiss on him. "How far is your house?"

"A couple of miles."

Far enough.

She ran her hand up the inside of his thigh as he pulled away from the curb, feeling the tough denim fabric against her fingers. And then tracing the hard outline of his cock as she got higher. She reached for his belt buckle.

He gave her a quick, startled glance. "What are you doing?"

"Eyes on the road." She pulled his zipper down. His cock, when she pulled it out, was heavy in her hand, already half hard and getting more so by the second. She let out a long, uneven breath. "Drive carefully," she told him, and unfastened her seatbelt so that she could lean across and put her mouth on him.

She'd always loved giving blowjobs, that hard immediacy, that complete and utter connection to a man's arousal. It had been so long, though. Nerves warred with anticipation. And then the fascination took over. Brady's cock was long and stiff, thickest just below the head. She nuzzled it and it bobbled against her with urgency. Experimentally, she gave him a lick and was rewarded with the sound of his breath hissing in.

And she abandoned subtlety and slid it into her mouth, taking him deep and fast so that she wrenched a groan out of him.

HE WAS GOING TO LOSE IT right there, Brady thought. Thea slid his cock in and out of the liquid warmth and it was all he could do to keep from nudging his hips toward her. And he was glad it was late at night with only a handful of cars on the road because suddenly he didn't give a damn about his lane or his signals or anything but the slick wet heat of her mouth and the way her tongue wrapped around his shaft with every bob of her head, stroking along the underside of his cock, inching him closer and closer to orgasm with every motion.

She wrapped her hand around his shaft and squeezed and he groaned again. And then she started to suck, keeping her head still, running her hand up and down.

And god, it was all he could do to hold on. He concentrated on the road and he recited batting averages in his head and the peaks of the Cascades and named every type of hop and malt he knew because there was no way, *no way* he was going to let himself come before he'd gotten her home, before he'd watched her face as she'd orgasmed, before she was underneath him, naked, abandoned and wrapped around him. Before he'd buried himself deep inside her.

There would be time, he thought, grinding his teeth as he drove up to his house. There would be time for everything.

Provided his molars held out.

Then he was turning off the engine and gingerly easing his aching cock back into his jeans.

The house was dark but he didn't care. All he was looking for was to get inside as quickly as possible. It needed to happen fast.

More. The demand drummed in his temples as they went through the side door. Moonlight streaming through the windows formed silver trapezoids on the linoleum of a kitchen floor.

"Roommates?" she asked as he led her into the living room with its broad bay window.

"Not unless you count my kayak."

"Good." And she flowed up against him, sliding her hands up under his shirt, ravenous for the feel of his body.

"You were so hot tonight. I saw you out there dancing and I thought I was going to die," Brady whispered against the side of her throat. "All I could do was watch you move and think about what you'd look like if you were out of this dress."

He trailed his fingertips around her shoulders to the nape of her neck where the red silk came together. His lips licked her collarbones. "And what you would say if I just started undoing it." He heard the growl of the zipper and felt her shiver as his fingertips traced the sliver of exposed skin. He purposely slowed his touch, made it excruciatingly slow and deliberate, as though he had all the time in the world.

She made an impatient noise.

He slipped his fingers inside the open back of her dress. "What's your rush? We've got all night."

SHE COULDN'T TELL HIM that her rush was because she was unable to believe it was real, that she wanted to experience it all before she woke up and realized it was all a dream. That was how it always went. She had girlfriends like Delaney who talked about the orgasms they had in their dreams. It never worked that way for Thea. Oh, sometimes she'd dream of arousal, maybe even of kissing or touching a man. The urgency would build, the anticipation. And then, somehow she'd find herself somewhere else and they'd be gone, no matter how hard she looked, leaving her to wake, empty and wanting.

But Brady's hands were on her, his fingers tracing the widening triangle at the back of her dress as the fabric fell away. And finally it was completely open, loose against her. He teased them both, his fingertips tracing the groove of her spine, the point where her back flared out to the rounded curve of her ass. And then he slipped his hands up the front of her, tracing over her flat belly, over the slight rise of breasts and into the deep vee of skin revealed by the neckline of her dress.

Thea shivered. He felt goose bumps rise in the wake of his fingertips as they brushed over the sensitive skin. He bent down and traced the line of her neck with the tip of his tongue, searching out the hollow at the base of her throat.

She ran her fingers up into his hair. And with a quick shrug of her shoulders, sent the dress slipping down her arms and cascading to the floor.

"OH, HONEY." And Brady's mouth went bone dry. There was the pool of red fabric on the floor and there was Thea, wearing nothing else save a ridiculously small scrap of something silky at her hips and her red stilettos. She was long and lean and lovely, sleek and strong and slightly curved. And he wanted to just stare because she was so beautiful, he wanted to devour her, run his hands and tongue over every inch of her at the same time. So he stood, helpless, while she gave one of those knowing smiles, those female smiles of wisdom as old as the hills and walked forward to slide her fingers under his shirt.

"I think you're overdressed." She circled around behind

him. "Yes, definitely overdressed," she murmured and pulled his shirt off over his head.

And then he felt her move up to press her bare breasts against his back and he swore the top of his head was going to blow off. Thea gave a throaty laugh at the noise he made and stepped away. "Now who's impatient?" She trailed her fingers down his lats as she moved away. "Anyway, I don't know what you're so upset about. You're the one who's behind. Maybe you ought to get out of those jeans."

She turned around and walked over to flop down on the couch, lying flat with her arms crossed under her head and her legs kicked up over the arm, those mile-high red heels still on.

Brady watched her a minute, poleaxed.

"I'm waiting," she said.

Galvanized into action, he stripped off the rest of his clothes and crossed to the couch. Now he was the one who was shaking, out of eagerness. He didn't know where to start. He wanted every bit of her at once.

THEN SHE LOOKED UP at him, dark-eyed and tempting, and bit her lip. "Are you going to touch me or do I need to do it myself?" she asked, sliding her fingertips down her throat.

Brady dropped to his knees beside the couch and put his hand over hers to stop it. "I think I can take it from there."

And he did know how to take it, she thought, closing her eyes to better savor the sensations as he licked his way down her chest and over the slight curve of her breasts. The strands of his hair trailed over her skin, making her shiver, making her nipples ache to be touched. He took his time, though, kissing his way inward in a spiral, making her wait, lingering over it while he traced circles over her other breast with his fingertips.

Now it was she who made the inarticulate noise of need. But he wouldn't be hurried. Instead, he circled his way slowly up the peaks and she watched as her nipples transformed to hard red beads, watched her breasts swell.

Then she closed her eyes and lay her head back to feel as he drew first one nipple, then the other into the wet heat of his mouth, rubbing with his tongue, biting lightly with his teeth to send the sharp twinge through her, followed by slick caresses that had her arching and gasping.

And he moved lower then, tracing his tongue across her belly, kissing, roving at will.

And lower still.

He shifted to press his mouth between her legs, moving them apart with his hands. Her heart hammered like it was trying to work its way out of her chest. Open to him, touch, sight, taste, scent. The skin of her inner thighs was hypersensitive. She felt the brush of his beard, the heat of his breath.

And then his mouth was on her.

Shocking in its heat. Overwhelming in its suddenness. No matter how she'd imagined, how she'd expected, she was nowhere close to the vivid immediacy. His mouth was on her, against her, searching out the most intimate part of her.

Making her gasp.

He didn't tease, he didn't make her wait now. He found her with his tongue. Just one touch was enough to have her crying out. But there was more, oh, more as he leaned in, tracing maddening patterns over her clit, stroking it again and again, sending her jolting against him, her hips moving helplessly, her head thrashing back and forth.

Insistent, unrelenting, he took her up until she was

wound tight with tension, until every slick caress sent heat washing through her, until she didn't think she could stand any more. She was poised on the edge, where sensations and senses merged until it seemed as though she could see vivid rainbows of color at his touch, the shades growing darker and more intense until suddenly she was flung over the edge in a wash of blinding white and an intensity of sensation that had her crying out and shuddering and shaking.

It seemed long moments later that it ended. Brady straightened. "Come on," he whispered and took her hand to pick her up off the couch.

His arms were warm around her. She barely noticed the hallway, the bedroom they entered. All she could see was the bed. When he laid her down on it and stripped off her thong, she shivered. He ran a possessive hand down her hip, over her thigh and calf and down to her stiletto. "Nice shoes," he murmured, kissing her. Thea reached for the straps at her ankles.

"Uh-uh." He put a hand over hers. "Leave them on." And then slipped onto the bed beside her.

The feel of his naked body was blissful, extravagant, a warm luxury. For a moment, she didn't move, still absorbing the sensation in a sort of giddy disbelief. There was something glorious about closing her eyes to savor his weight against her as she sank back onto the mattress.

He leaned over to his bedside bureau. There was a crackle of foil as he sheathed himself. Then he poised himself over her, his face taut now with the need for control. She felt the startling slip of his cock against her still sensitive clit as he rubbed himself through the slickness. She looked up into his face. Anticipation threaded through her.

The time for finesse was gone. His eyes were hot, dark, driven.

Desperate.

"I want to be in you," he whispered.

And with a sudden thrust of his hips, he was.

Thea cried out blindly. There was nothing like this, no sex toy, no vibrator, nothing that could make her feel this completeness, this connection, this reality. Hot and hard and silky soft and insistent, he was all the way inside her, filling her completely. His body surged against her, as much force as flesh, making her feel every least fraction of motion. And he went deep, so deep it wrenched a cry from her every time he sank himself home.

The sensation overwhelmed her. She'd thought about it over the years, tried to remember what it was like. Nothing had prepared her for the reality. She wrapped her arms around him, her fingers slipping on the muscles that bunched and tightened with the motion.

And he watched her, his eyes narrowed with pleasure.

She'd wrapped her legs around his waist but it wasn't enough. She wanted to feel him deeper. She worked them up higher, around his sides. And finally, higher still, over his arms to rest her ankles on his shoulders. Turning his head, he kissed her instep, then he looked down and his eyes darkened.

She could see. If she glanced down where they came together, she could see it all, the thick shaft of his cock, sliding in and out of her. And it was incredible, suddenly so real. "Oh, Brady," she said softly. "Look at it."

AND HE DID—at her face, her breasts, the long sweep of torso down to where they were intimately joined. But it wasn't that that overwhelmed Brady. It was the excitement and arousal in Thea's voice, the fascination in her eyes. "I want you to come," she whispered. "I want to feel it, I want to see it."

"Not yet," Brady ground out. "Not until you do."

"I already did," she purred. And when she brought one of her hands down to caress her own breast, squeezing it with obvious pleasure, that was it. Too much. More than he could take, the sight, the sound, the scent, the sensation. He pumped into her again and he could feel it starting, could feel himself go past the point of inevitability, his curse turning into a groan as he felt the rumble and gather and tightening and he poured himself into her.

It took a moment before he could do anything more than breathe and hold himself feebly on his elbows. Thea slipped her legs down so that he could roll onto his back beside her.

"What's wrong?" She frowned at him in concern. "The condom didn't break, did it?"

"No. I just came."

"I noticed." She kissed him. "I liked it. Didn't you?"

He felt the bliss spread over his face. "Oh yeah. But it seems to me like you missed out on the deal." He traced his fingers over her torso.

"You were in the room too, right?"

"Yeah."

"I wasn't speaking in tongues to stroke your ego."

"But you didn't come."

"I already did earlier, when you were going down on me."

"But not when I was in you."

She moved her shoulders. "I don't, at least not that way. Female anatomy, honeybunch. The right parts aren't in the right place for some of us. That doesn't mean it doesn't feel amazing, though," she added, thinking about the exquisite sensation of being *filled,* being stroked so completely. "Of course, if you really feel bad about it, I have a few ideas for ways you could make it up to me."

"I'll get right on it, as soon as I can move. Keep those shoes on." He winked. "We'll see what we can do."

4

SHE ROSE OUT OF SLEEP as if she was coming to the surface of a pool. One moment, she was swimming through the province of dreams, her body heavy and languid, her mind floating free. The next, sleep was releasing her to rise up ever more rapidly to consciousness, first awareness of self, then mind, then body.

The mattress beneath her was soft. She moved to shift, but something impeded her. Not something, she realized, someone. A male someone.

And the memory of the night before came rushing back.

Stifling a groan, Thea opened her eyes. Daylight streamed into an unfamiliar room. Accordioned paper shades at the windows, mismatched furniture, blue throw rug on the hardwood floor. Propped against the dresser was a kayak paddle. Opposite the bed, looking out of place, hung a surprisingly beautiful black-and-white photo of a high waterfall cascading from a cliff's edge.

She didn't know whether to sigh or grin. It had been real, every second of it. For the first time in seven years she had done the deed, and it was true what they said about bicycles.

It all came back.

And then a fatuous grin did spread over her face. It had been nothing if not amazing, amid the feeling of unreality that persisted over the fact that she'd done it at all. Especially given that it had been with a guy she barely knew. The key was not to spoil it by letting morning kill the fantasy. Time to get moving.

Tentatively, she shifted to get loose. The arms around her tightened and he made a sleepy noise of protest. Not he, Brady, she recalled. That was something, anyway. She may have slept with an almost complete stranger but at least she had a name. She made a more determined effort to get loose.

"Wher' goin'?" he mumbled, eyes still closed.

"Go back to sleep," she whispered. "I'll see you around."

He tightened his arms, eyes still closed, but he moved over to kiss her. "Stay."

"I can't."

He slid one hand up over her breast. "Gotta date?"

"No."

"What's the hurry?"

"I've got to get going."

Instead of releasing her, he closed his lips over her breast. The liquid heat stunned her for a moment. His hand slid up over her other breast. "You've got to get going?" he murmured, licking her nipple, then pressing it lightly with his teeth. "I think I can help with that."

A wave of pleasure washed over her so that for a moment, all she could do was relax back against the pillow. "Mmm."

"Oh yeah." His hand slid slower, over her ribs, along her waist, over her hip. "Yep, I think I can get you going."

Thea struggled to keep from being engulfed by that mindless tide of pleasure. "I didn't mean it that way."

"I did," he said, switching his mouth to her other breast. The overnight stubble on his chin scraped lightly over her skin, bringing every nerve to attention. "It's Saturday morning. You're supposed to relax." His hand crept lower.

"I have a class at one."

"Oh, we've got a lot of time until then." He shifted to begin licking his way down her belly.

There was something about the heat and the warmth, the light strokes of his fingers over her thighs counterpointed by those determined lips moving ever farther south that was making it impossible to protest. He shifted, shrugging the sheet out of the way, and moved between her thighs. She caught her breath. "Look—"

"Oh, I'm looking," he assured her.

"I really need to—"

And then his mouth found her and the words turned into an incoherent noise. "I know what you need to do."

This wasn't how one-night stands were supposed to go, she thought feverishly. They were supposed to be hot and fast and furious.

And over.

She was supposed to wake up full of regrets, he was supposed to want her gone and they were both supposed to go their separate ways as soon as possible.

Clear idea in principle. But his mouth was determined and persuasive and she found herself losing her focus under the seductive assault of his tongue. Anyway, what did it really matter? What would sex in the morning do that it hadn't the night before, except give her more of that mind-blowing pleasure? After all, it had been almost too many years to count since she'd had an orgasm in the presence of anyone besides herself. Who knew how long it would be before she did it again? She might as well get it while the getting was good.

And oh, it was good. She caught her breath as he slid two fingers inside her and then she stopped thinking at all. The only thing that mattered was the motion and the gathering tension, that divinely torturous sensation that made her equally desperate to reach the climax and desperate to stretch it out as long as possible.

The phone rang and she jolted, eyes flying open.

Brady raised his head. "Oops, sorry, forgot to unplug."

"Shouldn't you get that?"

"That's why I've got the machine." He bent to her again.

"Someone's calling," she protested but not all that strongly. She couldn't really make herself care, not when she could feel her own heat forming under his mouth, feel the incipient orgasm like a swelling bubble within her that was just about to—

The machine beeped. "Brady, Michael. Pick up the damned phone. I need you here, now. We've got an emergency."

CURSING, BRADY VAULTED for the phone. "Michael? What's going on?"

For once, Michael didn't sound calm and controlled. He sounded rushed and agitated and—getting Brady's immediate attention—frightened. "It's Lindsay. She's bleeding."

Lindsay, Michael's wife. Lindsay, who was four months pregnant with twins. "What's going on?"

"We don't know. We're taking her to the ER but I need someone to watch the kids. How fast can you get here?"

"Ten minutes," he promised, watching Thea dress. Regret warred with concern.

"I'm leaving the kids with our neighbor, Paula. You remember where the spare key is, right?"

"Don't worry about it," Brady said, buttoning his jeans.
"Go take care of Lindsay. I'm on it."

"I'll call when I know what's going on." In the background, a dispatch radio crackled.

"Where are you?"

"Out by the ambulance."

This was getting spooky. "Okay, go. And Michael—"

"What?"

"I hope everything's okay."

THEA STOOD on Robyn's porch, fumbling for her key. She was sure there were more ridiculous things to be wearing at 8:00 a.m. on a Saturday morning than her flashy tango dress, but she wasn't sure she could think of one offhand. With a sigh of relief, she stepped inside and closed the door behind her. Definitely relief, no sneaking regrets about the interruption in there. She didn't think. Okay, maybe a tiny regret, but really, what would one more round of sex have meant?

Another two or three orgasms?

Impatiently, she quashed the voice in her head. The last thing she needed was another guy who wouldn't take no for an answer, however fun his persuasion was. She should be relieved that he'd gotten that phone call.

Robyn shuffled out of the back in her bathrobe, hair still wet from her shower. Darlene jostled her way past to jump around Thea.

"How's my girl? How's my girl?" Thea asked, bending down to rub the sturdy little body. Darlene wriggled in doggie ecstasy, making a low moaning noise as Thea began rubbing her ears.

"Come on, Darlene, time to go out," Robyn said, but the dog ignored her. Robyn sniffed. "Some loyalty."

"Dogs are like guys," Thea said wryly. "Rub them in the right place and they're yours."

Robyn laughed. "So, what happened to you at the *milonga?* One minute I saw you dancing and the next you were walking away."

She'd never called. Thea closed her eyes. "Oh Robyn, I'm so sorry, I didn't even think. I just got distracted."

"Yeah, I know." Robyn yawned. "I saw you guys kissing on the river walk. When you didn't come back, I sort of figured what was going on." She tightened the sash of her robe. "Besides, I was kind of busy myself."

"Oh really?" Thea said. "And just who were you busy with?"

"Raoul."

"The Latin lover? This I've got to hear."

"You first."

Now it was Thea's turn to yawn. "Priorities. Caffeine first or I won't be able to stay awake long enough to talk. Do you want to make it or shall I?"

Robyn shook her head. "I have a better idea. Let's go get breakfast and compare notes. We need coffee and Darlene needs a walk. Make sense?"

"Love it. Ten minutes," Thea promised.

It took more like fifteen, but Robyn wasn't a stickler for technicalities. They walked down to a café called Stella's to sit under the spreading shade of the maples and order Belgian waffles, plus a corn muffin for Darlene.

"It's her favorite kind," Robyn said.

"Really."

"Really. We've done a thorough study of it. Date nut was a contender for a while, but corn eventually swung the day."

Beside them, Darlene sat up alertly, swinging her blunt head back and forth at the scents wafting through the air.

Thea took a happy gulp of coffee. "Okay, you first. So what happened?"

Robyn poured water into Darlene's bowl and settled back. "Ah, Raoul, the last of the red-hot lovers."

"That bad, huh?"

"That bad. You know, I've always watched those hips and that mouth and figured he'd be pretty tasty when he let loose. You know what a flirt he is and he has that Bambi-eyes thing going."

Thea raised her brows. "I'm hearing a 'but' here. Bad sex?"

"You know how he dances like he's more focused on himself than on his partner? Well, that's kind of how he has sex, too. Not on whether he was feeling good, but how he looked doing it. He wanted to do it in front of the mirror, which was cool—until I realized he was watching himself."

"Ouch."

"Yeah, well, never make the mistake of bringing the guy home. When you're at their place, you can always leave. Then again, you have to deal with their bathrooms," she added thoughtfully.

"There's that," Thea agreed, lips twitching.

The waitress set their plates before them. Darlene began quivering but didn't move from her seat. Robyn winked at Thea. "Corn muffin," she said, stripping off the wrapper and setting it down for Darlene to devour.

In the time it took Thea to blink, the muffin was gone. "Wait a minute. Where did…?" Before her, the pavement was clean and Darlene was sniffing the ground for crumbs.

"Light speed, that girl." Robyn pulled her plate toward

her. "So anyway, you know my story. What happened with you? Last I saw, you were walking off with the mystery man. Who was he?"

"Oh, just some guy who stopped at the dance."

Robyn gave her a delighted grin. "After how many years of being sidelined, you went off and slept with some guy who walked by the *milonga?*"

"Don't rub it in, you'll take away my appetite," Thea groaned.

"You should get double Belgian waffles for this. Honey, I'm proud of you. So how was it?"

"Fabulous. Of course, probably all sex is fabulous when you've done without for as long as I have," Thea added dryly. "But I don't care. It was great. *He* was great. Funny and sweet and…inventive," she decided. "And he has these really great hands, really big and strong hands, and—"

"And does this guy have a name? Besides Love God?"

"Brady, but it doesn't matter. It was a one-night stand." She frowned and began slicing into her waffle.

"Ah. One of those," Robyn said wisely. "Did he turn into a jerk this morning?"

"No."

"But he kicked you out."

He hadn't kicked her out. He definitely hadn't kicked her out, Thea thought, shivering at the memory of him licking her thighs.

"Earth to Thea."

She glanced up to find Robyn watching her. "What? Oh, yeah. Um, no, he wasn't rude or trying to get rid of me or anything."

"Then why'd you run away so fast? I don't get it. I mean, you got back here at like eight o'clock. The only reason I was alone was because I shoved Raoul out the door last night when we were through."

Thea toyed with the berries on her waffle. "I thought it would be better if we left a one-night stand a one-night stand."

"Meaning?"

"D is for done."

"And what did he think?"

"He was sort of lobbying for the bed and, ahem, breakfast angle." She cleared her throat. "If you know what I mean."

Robyn stared. "And you left why?"

"He got a phone call. Family emergency. It seemed like a good time to go."

Seeming to accept that, Robyn took a bite of waffle and chewed. "So where'd you leave it? Are you guys going to get together again?"

"I doubt it." Thea made little crosshatch patterns in her whipped cream with her fork.

"Why? Didn't he ask for your number?"

"Well…"

"Well what?"

Thea coughed. "I kind of left while he was in the bathroom."

"What the hell did you do that for?"

"I didn't want to be hanging around," she blurted. "You know what I mean, like a room service guy waiting for a tip? I hate that."

"So you bolted."

"Robyn, it doesn't matter. It's not like it was going to turn into anything anyway. It was a quickie. I don't know what got into me."

"Don't hand me straight lines like that, sugar."

Thea rolled her eyes but a smile tugged at the corners of her mouth. "It's like meeting a guy in a bar. Real life relationships don't start that way."

"Not if you run off, they don't."

"You know what I mean."

Robyn's gaze was intent. "This guy made you laugh. You had a good time. I don't see what's so wrong with exploring the minutest ghost of a chance that you might go out."

"I don't even live here."

"So? That didn't stop you last night."

"Last night was…"

"What?"

"I don't know." Thea's voice was aggrieved. "I just know if I wind up dating again—"

"If?"

"If," she repeated. "If I do, this time I'm going to do it right. I'm not going to dive into something before I know who the guy is. I'm going to find out what he's all about. Make sure the charming quirks aren't the first hints that he's a psycho. And then maybe, if everything seems okay, I'll…"

"Yes?"

"Have coffee with him." She forked up a berry.

"What a wild woman. You know, this smart, deliberate thing is all well and good, but it doesn't account for chemistry."

"And chemistry's done what for me?"

Robyn waggled her eyebrows.

"Besides that. Have you forgotten my track record? I have a genius for picking guys who are either bums or psychos, thank you very much, Dad."

"You're mellowing. Two years ago, you'd have told me that guys were all bums and whack jobs, period."

"I've watched my girlfriends." She reached down to rub Darlene's ears. "I'm willing to admit that there might, just might be some good ones out there. But I don't think I'm going to find one by jumping in the deep end. You're supposed to get to know them first, decide you care about them, *then* sleep with them."

"Jeez, Thea, it's not like if you see him again it means you're bonded for life. It's like shopping—you try things on, you don't necessarily buy them. Sometimes it's for fun, you know? Get back in practice. Get used to having orgasms again."

"I suppose."

"I suppose? We're talking about orgasms, here."

"Okay, maybe you're right. Next time."

"I don't suppose you're willing to take another run at Love God, there."

"Next time," Thea said firmly.

The waitress stopped at their table with a tray. "Here we are, ladies, two mimosas."

Thea blinked. "We didn't order these."

"I know. They're compliments of the gentlemen over there."

Thea glanced over to see a pair of guys at another table nod at them.

"Well, how about that," Robyn said. "What a nice thing to do. Isn't that nice, Thea?"

Looking at her suspiciously, Thea nodded.

Robyn raised her glass and touched it to Thea's. "Well, I'd call that a sign." She held up her glass in a toast to

their admirers, who were already rising. "Welcome back
to the fray."

THE WHOLE UNCLE THING had taken Brady by surprise. He
liked it. He hadn't expected to but he did, a lot. Little kids
were fun. Well, except for the diaper part. He could pass on
the diaper part. Mostly, though, being an uncle was cool.

At least until the whole horsey rides thing got started.
It was one thing for Drew, who wasn't even two, but
Cory had turned three the month before, and then he got
the bright idea of both of them riding at the same time,
and after two hours of horsey rides with little heels
drumming his sides and little hands pulling at his hair,
Brady was starting to feel like he'd been hiking all day
with a seventy pound pack. Which, in a way, he supposed he had.

"Okay, podners, time for Trigger to go back to the stable."

"Who Trigger?" Cory wanted to know as Brady paced
around to the couch so they could scramble off.

"Sounds like your Daddy's neglecting your education."
He didn't stand up, just stayed down on the carpet and
leaned against the front of the couch with a sigh.

Cory and Drew, meanwhile, were jumping up and down
on the couch like it was a trampoline. At least it was soft,
Brady figured wearily.

"Wanna play!" Cory demanded.

After almost two hours, Brady had regrettably exhausted
his repertoire. They'd already played Lego, blocks, elevator,
shadow puppets—and horsey. Brady was fresh out of in-
spiration.

"Wanna play," Cory said again.

Brady racked his brain. In a normal house, he could

put in a video but Lindsay didn't let them watch much TV. He spied his backpack and thought fast. "Cards?" he asked, rising to get it. Cards could be educational, he thought wildly. Numbers, shapes, colors, memory games. He pulled out his deck. There had to be something they could do.

"So how about a little Texas hold'em, huh?" He shuffled the cards. "You got any money?"

"Got any money?" Cory echoed.

He kept them entertained for a good half hour, though his "pick a card, any card" trick was underappreciated in his estimation.

"Wanna play." Cory repeated the refrain that had begun to give Brady the twitches. He set the deck down.

"Tell you what, buddy. We'll play, but first, why don't you go into the kitchen and tell me what time it is?"

Cory scrambled off the couch and raced across the room. Drew, following his big brother as always, tripped and fell. A wail rose from him. Resignedly, Brady levered himself up and walked over. "Hey, come on dude, you're okay. Here, let's get up." He raised Drew to his feet and inspected him. Outside of a bright red face screwed up into tears, all his parts appeared to be in the same place as usual.

"The big hand's on the eight and the little hand's on the eleven," Cory reported breathlessly.

Eleven-forty, almost three hours after he'd gotten the call.

"I want Mommy," Drew wailed, weeping afresh.

"It's gonna be okay," Brady said lamely, boosting his nephew up. In reality, he hadn't a clue. So far, no call from Michael, anyway, which left him wondering uneasily what was going on. Women didn't die from pregnancy complications, did they? He just didn't know. There was one whole heck of a lot of stuff he didn't know. Then again, he suspected that a guy couldn't live long enough to learn the full handbook on women, especially since they each had their own. Not only how they ticked but how their minds worked. *Especially* how their minds worked.

Like Thea.

Beautiful and able to move like no woman he'd ever met. Acerbic enough to make him laugh. They'd had a good time, he'd thought. Shoot, they'd had a great time. So why had she been in the big rush to leave? More to the point, why had she left while his back was turned, without even a note or a number? It bugged him, and Brady wasn't usually a guy to get bugged by much. Live and let live was his motto.

He wasn't sure he'd be able to stick with that in this case.

There was a sound at the door and Michael walked in. "Hey, guys."

"Daddy!" Cory raced over to him.

"Daddy," Drew cried, waving his arms.

With profound relief, Brady walked up to Michael and handed Drew over.

"What happened here?" Michael asked, glancing at the tearstained cheeks.

"He tripped on the carpet. The scars shouldn't show much once he's grown."

"Thanks for the good news." Michael bounced Drew a little and rubbed Cory's hair, but strain hovered around his mouth and eyes. "So what have you been up to?" His gaze drifted to the cards on the coffee table.

"Counting," Cory informed him, jumping up and down. "Four, five, six, seven, eight, nine, ten, jack, queen, king."

Michael gave Brady a hard look. "What have you been teaching them?"

"Got any money?" Cory asked.

"I can explain," Brady said quickly.

"I hope so."

"Look, how's Lindsay?"

"They're keeping her overnight for observation." Michael let Drew slip down. "Thanks for taking over."

"Not a problem. Any time, you should know that."

Michael scrubbed his hands through his hair. "Mom and Dad are visiting Keeley this weekend. I didn't know who else to call."

"So, do you know what's going on?"

"Well, she's going to be okay. The babies are okay, too."

Brady let out a breath and more tension than he knew he'd been holding onto. "Good news."

"Yeah, good news. I didn't know what to think this morning. There was blood everywhere, it seemed like. Wigged me out."

It was enough to make a guy swear off the wife and family thing altogether, Brady thought. Bad enough to deal with the labor part of it, but the panic and powerlessness of knowing something was deeply wrong with the person you cared about most and you couldn't do a thing about it? He'd stick with kayaking, he decided. "Want coffee?"

"No. I've been sucking it down for the last couple of hours, waiting for the doctors and the tests." Michael shook his head and went into the kitchen. "Nerve-racking as hell."

"So what's the story? What's wrong?"

"The short version is placental abruption."

"Oh, well, hell, I could have told you that."

"Funny." He tossed Brady a Coke and took one for himself, and then as an afterthought grabbed juice boxes for the boys. "Her placenta's detaching from the uterus. Fortunately not too much or we'd have lost the babies and maybe her. As it is, things'll be okay, they think. They want to keep her a couple of days to make sure it's fine but after that she can come home."

"Well, that's good," Brady said, cracking open his Coke.

Michael poked the straw in Drew's juicebox and handed it to him. "I do," Cory demanded, reaching for his. Michael shrugged and passed it down. "That's not all. They want her on bed rest until the delivery."

"Bummer."

"Life's going to be different."

"I guess. That's what, four months she's got left?"

"Five."

"Yeah. You don't take a woman who just ran the Portland marathon and tell her to lie around for five months. Better lay in a supply of DVDs," Brady advised.

"She'll get through it. She's scared enough for the twins that she'll do whatever they tell her to."

Brady nodded and glanced down. "Hey, you need some help?" He crouched down to help Cory, who was trying with great concentration and without much success to get his straw to puncture his juicebox.

"Me," Cory said stubbornly.

"Got to get the straw out of the wrapper, my man," Brady said, slipping off the plastic and handing the tube to Cory.

"Get ready for some changes. For starters, we're going to have to jettison the theater."

Brady stared up at Michael. *"What?"*

"Total bed rest for five months, Brady. I mean everything. No cooking, no cleaning, no taking care of the kids, no nothing."

"No sex?"

"You're not funny."

"Sorry. Maybe you should get a nanny. Delegate."

"This is my family," Michael said. "I don't delegate. I'm barely going to be able to keep up with the properties we've got. No way am I going to be able to take on developing the theater, as well."

Brady rose. "But I've got the concept, Michael, and it's killer. Tango. We do it as a dance theater. You know, performances, lessons."

"Line dancing at eight?"

Brady shot him a withering look. "You know what I mean."

"It's not going to happen. C'mon, guys," Michael said to the boys, and headed out of the kitchen.

Brady followed him. "So, what, you're going to let it sit there for five months? Can we afford that?"

"No way, we can't afford that." Michael continued down to his bedroom. "It'll eat up half the money we've earmarked for construction. By the end of five months, we won't be able to finish it anyway. We're going to have to pull out."

"We can't pull out." Not when he could already see it taking shape in his mind's eye. Not when he knew it would be a success. "We'll never get a property like this again," he protested.

"Brady, I can't do it. I don't have the bandwidth." He ducked into the closet.

"Delegate. Hire subcontractors."

Michael came out with an overnight bag, glowering. "I've got a better idea, smart guy. You want it so much, you hire the subcontractors."

Brady blinked. He could feel the breeze blowing into his open mouth. "Me?"

"Yeah, you." Michael gave a sardonic smile. "Pulling out looks a whole lot better now, doesn't it?"

Brady narrowed his eyes. "No, it doesn't." He watched as Michael opened a couple of drawers before coming up with a nightgown. Pulling out was out of the question. Not going to happen. And if Michael couldn't do it, then that meant… "I'll do it."

"Yeah, right."

His tone was enough to make Brady bristle. "Hell yeah, right. Why not? How hard can it be, if I get the right people?"

"Dude, you have no idea." Michael crossed back to the closet to toss in Lindsay's robe and slippers. He headed to the bathroom to rifle through drawers, unearthing a brush and squinting at bottles of lotion. "Moisturizer, cleanser," he muttered. "I don't know what this stuff is."

"Then I guess you'll have to figure it out. Like I will," Brady added. "I make beer for four different places. I ought to be able to handle a renovation."

Giving up, Michael tossed all of the bottles into the overnight bag and zipped it up. He turned to the hall. "Look, I've got to get back to the hospital. You want to do this, then do it. Just don't screw up, because I'm not going to have time to bail you out."

"I'm not going to need you to bail me out," Brady insisted.

"Good. Then we're all set." He bent down to give the boys hugs. "Daddy's got to go for a while but I'll be back and then we'll go to the park. Meantime, your uncle will be here."

He rose and looked at Brady. "And do me a favor, huh? Don't teach 'em to draw to an inside straight."

5

SHE LOVED TEACHING. Not that she didn't love the dance—of course she loved the dance—but there was something about watching a student go from staring blankly to mastering a figure that Thea found incredibly satisfying.

There had been a time she'd expected to dance for a living. That had been before she'd grown to nearly six feet and before she'd found out how much of a battle the life of a professional dancer was: the relentless auditions, the frenzied scuffle for work, the desperately low pay. And the long, long odds against success.

But then her dance instructor challenged her to choreograph a showcase and teach it to a performance team, and it was like coming home. Suddenly she knew her future—she would teach, she would choreograph. She'd be the driving force behind the performances.

Even when the lightning bolt had hit and she'd moved to New York, she'd continued taking daily classes to hone her craft. Back then, Robyn had been just another classmate with ambitions of Broadway glamour. Thea had been the one who'd wanted to teach.

Ironic that Robyn was the one who'd wound up with this, the dance studio, while Thea had quit modern and jazz dance entirely, all of it too bound up with what had happened in New York. She'd turned to tango and the *milongas* to satisfy what had once been her passion. She'd turned to tango and the *milongas* to satisfy her longing for the human touch.

Now, somehow, it felt as if she'd come full circle, as if she was back where she belonged. Stepping through the gap in the chest-high counter that separated the entry area from the ballroom was about more than stepping onto the pale, sprung wood floor. It was about returning to a life she thought she'd abandoned.

And it felt good.

Carla Petrocelli and Chuck Crocker weren't dance aficionados; they were there because Carla had a dream of waltzing in white at their wedding. And from the way Chuck looked at her, whatever Carla wanted, he'd do his damnedest to get, including private dance lessons. Beefy and a little awkward, Chuck stood in his U of O T-shirt, scrubbing at his cropped reddish hair. Carla was small and pinch-faced, but when she glanced at him, something about her glowed.

It made Thea smile. "All right. Let's put some music on and you can warm up. That'll give me an idea of what you know and we can go from there." And with a push of a button, the strains of "Moon River" filled the room.

Frowning with concentration, Chuck led Carla through the steps of a basic, lips moving as he counted for them both. Thea had to give him credit, he was keeping to something approximating waltz time—it just had nothing to do with the actual music playing. And yet they both looked happy, laughing when Chuck stumbled over Carla's toes, the reflections of their grinning selves replicated hundred-fold as they moved into the mirrored corner.

"Okay, let me give you the count. One-two-three, one-two-three, one-two-three," she said, clapping every count of one. Chuck, she was gratified to see, managed to get on the beat as they made the turn. Thea followed along with them. "Good, Chuck, that's great," she said as they headed back to the front and she turned after them. "One-two-three, one-two-three, one…"

And the words died in her throat.

Chuck and Carla moved blithely on, even as Thea stopped in the center of the ballroom floor, staring at the man she'd never expected to see again.

Brady.

He stood there watching her, arms folded on the white counter at the edge of the ballroom. She fought the urge to press her hands to her cheeks to cool them. With his disheveled blond hair and his crooked grin, he was more than enough to have her pulse speeding. And without warning she had a sudden, vivid flash of lying under him in bed, feeling his back muscles flex under her fingers as he stroked his—

Thea moved her head to ward off the memory. She'd left without a word. If positions had been reversed, she and her friends would have considered him the prince of jerks. What did that make her, and was he there to tell her that?

For that matter, how had he found her? The *milonga,* of course, she realized immediately. The name of Robyn's studio. And tracking down Robyn's studio meant tracking down her. In this web-enabled day and age, getting lost and staying that way wasn't as easy as it had once been.

He saw her looking and extended his index and middle finger in a peace sign. And grinned in enjoyment at her frown.

Flushing, Thea turned back to Chuck and Carla. Okay,

so rudeness aside, couldn't the guy take a hint? There had been a reason she'd gone. She didn't want him here. She didn't want to see him again, to deal with what she felt. It was too much, too soon.

And if he thought she was going to break off from her lesson to talk to him, he thought wrong. Robyn's students had paid for her time and her time they were going to get. "Okay," she said briskly. "Let's learn a new figure."

Drilling Chuck and Carla on first the man's part, then the woman's part individually until they got it took some time. Dancing through the steps with each one of them took more. And Brady stayed. A normal man would have gotten bored, or at the very least, tired. A normal man would have left long since.

Brady stood and watched.

Thea could feel the heat of his gaze on the back of her neck as she ran through the steps with Carla. Dancing with a woman didn't bother her. She'd long ago perfected the ability to hold her frame, arms rigid to keep their spacing, gaze aimed resolutely over the shoulder of her partner so that she could dance the step without eye contact. It came in handy when dealing with anyone she wanted to maintain a professional distance with, particularly students.

Of course, it wasn't Carla she was worried about.

Three quick steps in succession and a spin, then a pivot to promenade and presto, they'd made a left turn. Thea led it again and suddenly the figure began to flow.

"I think I've got it," Carla said in excitement.

"One more time," Thea suggested. Getting it was one thing; it was important to cement it. Three quick steps and turn, then pivot to promenade. Three quick steps and turn, then pivot and presto!

She was staring straight at Brady.

Who raised his eyebrows and pursed his lips, fanning himself like he was overheated.

She refused to be amused, Thea thought as she finished the step. "Okay, you two ready to give it a go?" she asked Chuck and Carla instead.

"We'll try," Chuck said.

Try being the operative word. Still, by the end of the lesson, they were running through it reasonably well. Thea fought the temptation to ask them to stay longer. "Good job," she told them. "A couple more weeks of this and you'll be ready to wow everyone."

Laughing, they walked off the floor to the entry area. And though she was tempted to stall and dry mop the floor with baby powder, she followed them. Granted, it was justifiable maintenance but she'd be putting off the inevitable, which was lame. Best to deal with Brady now and get it over with.

He watched her as she walked up, making her conscious of every step she took. She wore high-heeled dance shoes and a blue-violet wraparound skirt with a stretchy black tank top. Serviceable, especially in a ballroom that never managed to stay cool enough. It was her typical lesson outfit. She'd never thought much about the fact that the skirt stopped a couple of inches above her knees.

Until now.

"You're quite a teacher," he said as she drew near.

"Enjoying yourself?" She stopped, keeping the counter in between them, a nice, safe solid barrier.

"Yeah. Especially the hot girl-on-girl dancing."

She narrowed her eyes at him. "What are you doing here?"

"You disappeared. Figured I had to do something to

find you. Was it something I said?" The corner of his mouth quirked.

Thea pressed her palms down on the white countertop and tried not to think about how good that mouth had tasted. "With that phone call, it looked to me like you had plenty going on. I decided I'd get out of your hair."

"You forgot to say goodbye."

The shift of her shoulder wasn't quite a shrug. "We were pretty well done."

"I don't think so." He ran his fingertips over the back of her hand. Instantly, all her nerve endings went to the alert. When she moved her hand, he grinned. "So what is it with you? I thought we had a good time. I did, anyway." He gave her a wicked look. "And I'm pretty sure you did, too, unless you're really good at faking."

"I don't fake."

"I remember that."

There was the low bong of the downstairs door as the students for the next class began to arrive. Perfect. All she needed was an audience.

"Look, Brady, the other night was great but I don't usually do that kind of thing."

His smile widened. "I thought you did it pretty well."

She could feel her cheeks heat. "That's not what I meant. I don't usually sleep with strangers."

"All the more reason we should get to know one another."

The last thing she needed to do was to dive into one of her trademark bad relationships. She'd meant what she'd said to Robyn—if she was going to get involved, she was going to do it right, and not with a guy who already demonstrably didn't know how to take no for an answer. She'd been there too many times already. She wouldn't—

couldn't—let herself go there again. "Look, you seem like
a really nice person but I'm not looking to get involved in
something right now."

"Why not? Is there a guy?" He caught up her left hand
and inspected it.

She worked hard not to react even as he studied her. His
eyes were very green as he raised his brows.

"No ring. No husband, I guess. Boyfriend?" he asked.

"No."

"Girlfriend?"

She scowled. "Of course not."

"That makes two of us. So then what's the problem?"

She heard the door to the back studio at the far side of the
ballroom open. It would be Robyn and one of her students
coming out from their private lesson. In the entry area, the
dancers for the next class chatted as they put on their suede-
soled shoes. Time to end this quickly, Thea decided.

"There's not a problem, Brady. I'm simply not interested."

"Really?" He toyed with her fingers. "I don't think I believe that." When he leaned forward, watching her eyes
closely, her pulse began to speed. He couldn't kiss her, not
here, not in front of everyone.

And she shouldn't want him to.

"Nope," he said softly. "I definitely don't believe that."

Thea wet her lips. "Look, I don't have time to deal with
this. The next class is starting in about five minutes. You
shouldn't have shown up here."

"You didn't give me a whole lot of choice. I found you
where I could find you."

"I'm working," she said sharply.

"Teaching?"

"Robyn is. I'm assisting."

"Ready for some tango?" Robyn asked from behind her as though on cue. She stopped beside Thea, glancing at Brady. "Who's this?"

"Brady McMillan," he said easily, releasing Thea's hand to shake Robyn's. "Got room for me in your class?"

HE'D ALWAYS HAD A TENDENCY to leap into things. If it felt like a good idea, then he went with it, trusting to his head and body to get him through. As a result, he'd had some singular experiences. He'd pancaked a few times, too, but he figured that was the price of admission. Whatever the class was, he figured it was worth trying to fake his way through, especially if it gave him a chance to get close to Thea.

The sweet-faced blonde he assumed was Robyn looked at him. "Weren't you at the *milonga* last weekend?"

Brady nodded. "Gave me a taste for it."

"We're two weeks into the class," Thea pointed out. "You'll be behind, and anyway, it's intermediate level." She handed him a printed schedule. "Come back later."

"I can catch up if you give me some help," he said easily. She wasn't going to put him off. He'd seen her eyes darken when he'd taken her hand, felt her tremble. She could pretend she wanted nothing to do with him all she liked.

He knew better.

Thea sighed. "You don't even have a partner."

"Why don't you dance with him?" Robyn suggested. Something flickered in her eyes, a glint of mischief.

Thea stared at her as though she'd sprouted an additional head. "How am I supposed to help you in the class if I'm dancing with him? He's a beginner."

"And you can teach anyone. We don't turn away students. Take him into the back studio if you need to give him some extra attention."

Brady kind of liked the sound of that.

"Extra attention?" Thea choked.

"You're going to need to take some private lessons if you want to keep up with this class," Robyn added to Brady.

"Private lessons sound fine to me," he said.

He could practically see the air vibrating around Thea. It amused him. He wasn't sure what was going on with her but no way was he going to let a woman this hot and, well, intriguing slip away. It had been too good the other night between them. And if she'd woken up with reservations, she was just going to have to get over them.

He wasn't about to give up without more.

Oblivious or intentionally ignoring the situation, Robyn walked over to the stereo. "All right, everyone, I'm going to put on some music. Go ahead and warm up."

And Brady walked through the gap in the counter to Thea. "So? What are we waiting for?"

SHE HAD, THEA ACKNOWLEDGED, been outmaneuvered, and so neatly she hadn't even seen it coming. Sure, he'd had help from Robyn, who knew exactly what she was doing. The music began, the measured pulse of piano, the sultry moan of accordion. The dancers drifted across the room into position. Brady stood expectantly before her.

And Thea stepped forward into his arms.

She could tell herself she didn't want him when he was across the room. It was harder when she was fused to him, his inner thigh hard and strong against hers. If it had been the foxtrot or the waltz, where dancers stood at a distance, she would have been all right, but tango demanded intimacy, from the tight, breast-to-chest dance position to the close footwork. With a partner who was focused on the dance, the intimacy was about the two of them crafting the flow of the movement together.

With Brady, it had nothing to do with the dance.

Heat. She could feel it through his clothing and hers, and it drew her back to stolen hours in the darkness, lying against each other in bed. And under his clothes she could feel the flex and ebb of muscles. They were lean and taut, strong but not bulky. And she could feel his fingers pressed against her back, knew the sensations they could coax from her body.

She remembered.

"What are you doing here?" she demanded in a low voice.

"Learning tango, I hope," he said blithely.

"You're not here for tango."

"Then why am I here?" he asked and surprised her by leading her into the basic eight he'd learned at the *milonga*.

"Because you obviously can't take a hint. What is it, you showing up here, some kind of game?"

"I don't play games."

She back-led him through a turn. "Oh yeah? I think you're one of those guys who can't handle a woman saying no."

"I don't think you are saying no," he murmured, pressing her more tightly against him.

"Oh, take a look, buddy. Read my lips," she began. And without warning, they jolted up against another couple. Thea stumbled, clutching at Brady's shoulders. "Excuse me," she rushed to tell the couple they'd run into. "So sorry. We weren't watching where we were going."

"I'll say," Brady muttered in her ear. "You told me to watch your lips."

"Listen," she began furiously, "just because we boffed

our brains out—" The words hung in the silence as Robyn stopped the music. Thea glanced across the room full of people staring at them and flushed. "Sorry." She cleared her throat. "We're, ah, just going to go in the back and run through a few things."

"Have fun," Robyn said helpfully.

Brady followed Thea into the private studio, closing the door behind them. "Time for some extra attention?"

Thea stalked farther into the room, then whirled on him. "You've got no business here."

"Sure I do. It's a free country. What was your tango party all about if not to get new customers?"

"You're not here for tango."

"Who says I'm not? You're supposed to be teaching me."

"You came here to find me."

"What was I supposed to do?" he threw back, an edge to his voice. "You were the one who walked out, remember?" Behind him, the wall of mirrors threw their reflections back at them.

"Did it ever occur to you that I walked because I didn't want you finding me?"

"Yeah?" He tucked his hands in his back pockets and moved forward. "But the question is why."

"I don't owe you an explanation," she said hotly.

"After the night we had? I'd call it common courtesy."

Thea threw up her hands in frustration. "You know, ninety-nine percent of the guys in the world would be thrilled to have a one-night stand where the woman didn't expect anything. Why can't you be one of them?"

"Because I think anything that good deserves a rematch. Or at least a reason."

"Yeah, well, think again. You might want more. I don't."

"Oh yeah?" He stepped toward her, his voice deceptively reasonable.

"Yeah."

"All right, then. Done. Teach me to dance."

Her brows lowered. "Give me a break."

"Now who's not listening? Come on, teach me. That's what I'm paying for." He stopped before her and raised his hands, staring at her.

Thea worked her jaw in silence.

"Still waiting," he said mildly.

She stepped in and slid her hand over his shoulder. And that quickly, he pressed his palm flat on her back and pulled her in against him.

For a moment, they didn't move. Ignore it, Thea told herself. He was only pushing her for a reaction. She had news for him, though, she could stand it as long as he could. He wasn't going to get to her.

But with every second that passed, she became more and more aware of his body. With every second, she became more and more aware of the rise and fall of his chest, the feathering of his breath on her cheek, his mouth so close. She could hear each separate beat of her pulse in her ears.

She cleared her throat. "I thought you wanted to dance."

"I'm trying to get my frame right."

"Your frame's fine."

"You think? I'm thinking maybe I need to adjust it a little bit," he said, and pulled her in closer to him. "Don't tell me you don't want it," he murmured in her ear. "Don't tell me you don't remember what it was like because I can feel you shivering."

"The air conditioning's up too high," she threw back in desperation.

"Bull," he murmured, lowering his face toward hers. "Why are you so dead set on running away from this?"

She couldn't remember why. She knew there was a reason, knew that she needed to keep to it, but with his lips so close to hers, when she knew all the places he could take her, it was hard to make herself care.

And she began to tremble harder.

"It was good," he whispered against her lips. "You know it was, and you know you don't find it like that very often. And when you do, you don't up and leave." He brushed his mouth against hers.

Thea wasn't aware that she moaned until she heard it. She couldn't think about anything but that tempting brush of his lips that only made her want more.

And the moan was all it took for him to crush his mouth to hers.

It was like being on one of those instant start roller coasters, one minute still, the next minute racing up the first hill, overwhelmed by sensation. His mouth was hot and demanding, fueled by equal parts desire and frustration. His hands were hard against her. And she could try to ignore the way his body felt, but then there was the taste of him, sharp and male. And she could try to ignore the taste, but there was his scent. And even if she managed to ignore that, there was the heady feel of his mouth on hers, his tongue caressing, teasing.

And then she couldn't make herself ignore any of it but matched him demand for demand, mindlessly eager for just one more taste. She pressed herself against him, curling her arms around his neck, catching her breath as he slipped one hand up under her tank to cup her breast, squeezing the nipple through her bra. A tiny bolt of sensation that had her making a noise of impatience.

Out in the main room, the students erupted in laughter at something Robyn said. The sudden sound was enough to have Thea dragging herself back to reality. She pulled away from Brady.

"I've got to be out of my mind," she muttered, stalking away from him. "We're in a dance studio. Robyn's out there with a class."

"Relax. The door is closed."

"Like that makes a difference?"

"Versus doing it in front of everyone, yeah." He watched her. "Maybe we should go somewhere else."

"Maybe you should. I've got to help Robyn teach a class."

"What about after?"

"After, I go home. Alone," she emphasized. "Look, I couldn't care less if you don't like hearing the word no, deal with it. We are done."

"I don't think so."

Thea didn't bother to answer. She walked out of the studio into the main ballroom without a backward glance. Brady followed her to an open space in the corner. When he stood before her, she exhaled audibly and stepped into dance position with him, keeping her frame crisp and staring resolutely over his shoulder. If she tried hard enough, she could make herself not feel.

"Dance zombie," he said softly in her ear.

"What?"

"You're wearing your dance zombie face. Like when you were dancing with your students before. Just in case you're wondering, it doesn't fool me."

"I'm not trying to fool you."

"That's good, because we're going to have to see a lot of each other if I start taking lessons."

Her eyes flicked toward him. "What?"

"More lessons."

"Does the phrase when hell freezes over mean anything to you?" she asked pleasantly.

"I don't know," he said. "Me, I like things hot."

It seemed like forever, but eventually the class did end. Eventually, she released him to walk off the floor with the rest. And she knew it was cheap, but she fled to the ladies room, taking her time after. When she came out, Brady was nowhere to be seen.

Exhaling, she picked up her shoe bag and sat to change into her street shoes, ignoring the flare of tension between her thighs. So there was something physical between them. So what? She'd lived without the physical for a long time. She could live without this.

She was zipping shut her bag when the door to Robyn's office opened. And to her everlasting surprise, Brady and Robyn stepped out, laughing.

"Then it's a deal," he said, turning to shake hands.

"I look forward to it. Thea," Robyn called. "Come on over here. You need to hear about this. This is Brady McMillan."

"I already know," Thea muttered.

"As in the brewpub McMillans."

Thea blinked. "The Lincoln School?"

Robyn nodded. "Brady and his brother recently bought an old theater they're going to remodel as a hotel and pub. They're thinking about working it as a tango theater and they're looking for some help from us."

Robyn's eyes were practically incandescent with excitement. The McMillans, Thea remembered. The brothers with the Midas touch. "That sounds like good news for you."

"I'll have to tell you all about it. Brady wants to keep

taking lessons here, but he also needs help coordinating some showcases."

"We'll need to move on it soon," Brady put in. "The grand opening isn't that far away and there'll be a lot of planning to do."

"Like I said, the only problem is that I go on vacation Friday."

"We start construction this week. I'm going to need input on some of the specs, maybe a roughed-out program pretty soon. Isn't there anyone else who can do it?"

And they both looked at Thea. "I'll check into it and get back to you," Robyn told Brady and turned to Thea. "You and I should talk and hammer out a way to get Brady exactly what he wants."

Thea didn't have to look at Brady to know he was grinning at that.

"I should get going and let you two hash out the details," was all he said, though. "Get back with me this week sometime before you go, Robyn, all right?"

"Absolutely," she said warmly.

He shook hands with Robyn and merely winked at Thea. "Have a good night."

The minute the downstairs door bonged to signal he was gone, Robyn whooped. "This is it, this is it, this is it!" she shrieked, throwing her arms around Thea's neck. "I am so set. Oh, honey, I know you don't want to deal with him but pretty please, just while I'm gone, work with him. I really need this to go. I swear, I'll never ask you to do anything again if you do this. Promise me?"

"I promise," Thea said with a sinking feeling.

6

HE'D NEVER BEEN A GLUTTON for punishment, Brady thought as he carried his kayak out the door of his house. He'd never been the type who got off on rejection, no matter how gorgeous the woman doing the rejecting was. He generally tended to go after women who were interested in him, which fortunately happened more often than not.

So he couldn't understand why he couldn't get Thea Mitchell off his mind. She kept telling him she wasn't interested. Taking the hint would be smart. Except that he couldn't forget the way her eyes had widened when he'd taken her hand, the way she'd moved in his arms.

The way her mouth had come alive under his.

That thought alone made him get hard. The first night they'd been together there hadn't been any of the shadows, there hadn't been any of the reluctance. That night she'd been there all the way and it had been the next best thing to a life-changing experience for him.

And it made him want her, not just physically but all of her, the throaty laughter as they'd danced, the mischief in her eyes in his living room, the woman who told him the song of the tango in the night.

What he didn't understand was why since then she'd been shutting down every time things got started with them.

The physical buzz there was real, that much was obvious. So why did she keep pulling away?

And why did he keep finding himself compelled to go after her?

He wasn't one of those guys who was hung up on saving wounded birds. He wasn't the type who was fascinated by the dysfunctional. What he wanted, pure and simple, was the woman he'd met that first night, the one who held nothing back. And he could sense her there, he just couldn't figure out how to let her loose.

But he wasn't ready to give up, not yet.

Brady hoisted the kayak up on his shoulder and headed for his Jeep. For now, he'd do what he always did when he needed to think. He'd go somewhere and beat his body all to hell and knock every thought clean out of his head, and when he hit that haze of exhaustion in the aftermath, then he'd start thinking. And he'd figure it out.

He leaned the paddles up against his vehicle as a silver minivan pulled into the driveway and Michael got out. Brady glanced over and adjusted his watch. "Hey."

"Hey yourself." Michael shut the door and walked up.

Brady turned, kayak still on his shoulder. "How's Lindsay?"

"Better."

"Better is good." Brady watched his brother come to a stop, hands in his pockets. "You, on the other hand, are looking ragged around the edges there. Kids working you over?"

Michael snorted. "The kids, the pubs, keeping Lindsay down. I'm looking into cloning."

"I'd figure Lindsay would be the easy part."

"The problem is, she forgets. Or she says 'one quick

thing' and the next thing I know, she's mopping the kitchen floor and hauling laundry around."

"I always knew women hogged the housework because it was more fun."

"You want fun, come over any time," Michael invited.

"Yeah, I think I'll hit the river instead. Unless you want me to sit the boys again," he added.

Michael rolled his eyes. "Yeah, you sit for me again, Cory's going to be running a Texas hold'em home game for his playgroup."

"I'm teaching him valuable survival skills," Brady said with dignity.

"Is that what you call it?" Michael watched Brady hoist the kayak onto the roof rack. "Speaking of learning experiences, how's everything going? You need any help?" he asked, his voice elaborately casual.

"With what? The kayak?"

"With work."

Brady fastened the clamps on the kayak and pressed the stopwatch button on his sports watch. He checked the display. "A minute five," he said approvingly. "Pretty good."

"A minute five for what?"

"A minute five between when you got here and when you started grilling me. That's not bad, considering you made a special trip for it."

Michael's brows lowered. "I would have done it at one of the pubs but you weren't around. I should have realized it was because you had kayaking to do."

"It's because I was up brewing and pitching yeast until about two in the morning."

Michael shook his head. "Who was the guy who was talking to me about delegating again?"

"You're the one who's supposed to be delegating, here, remember?"

"Cut me some slack, will you? It's a new job for you, this is a new job for me, too."

"What is?"

"Watching. But if you've got time to go paddling on a weekday morning, you've probably got everything all set."

"Yep." Brady checked the kayak for stability and stepped away.

"Because, I figure you know we're on a tight schedule and if you needed help, you'd—"

"Say the words." Brady's lips twitched.

Michael stopped. "What?"

"Come on, Michael. Say the words."

"What are you talking about?"

"You want to know, you've got to say the words."

"Just an update. Just give me that much."

"An update on what?"

"The theater."

"Oh, the theater," Brady singsonged. "You mean the theater project that you passed off to me because you were supposed to be home taking care of the family? That project?" He tossed the paddles in the Jeep.

"Are you done listening to yourself talk?" Michael grumbled. "You want to tell me something worthwhile?"

Brady grinned. "Relax. Everything's fine."

"*Now* I'm worried."

"Look, you already had a budget and a schedule set. The architect and I put together a detailed work order yesterday—"

"You've already met with the architect?" Michael yelped.

"Two days ago."

"But—"

"Release, Michael." Brady caught him by the upper arms and began walking him toward his minivan. "Go to that happy place."

"I'm mainlining SpongeBob SquarePants. There is no happy place. At least tell me your theme," Michael pleaded.

"I already did. Tango."

"Be serious."

"I am. You know how big the dance community is here in this town? And look at all the ballroom dance stuff on TV. It's big business."

"It's a fad and it'll be gone in a year."

"Ballroom dance, square dance, folk dance." Brady opened the van door. "Before ballroom it was swing, before that it was line dances, before that it was disco. People love to dance. That's what we're tapping into. If they get tired of tango, we'll go to something else. Trust me. You didn't think a jail would work, either."

Michael gave Brady a suspicious look before getting in. "You're not doing it just to get next to the tango babe, are you?"

"I can get next to the tango babe on my own." At least he thought so. "Relax, Michael. I'll keep you up to date but this gig's mine."

"We're partners," Michael reminded him.

"And right now, partner, you need to focus on your family. Look, I've got a site meeting with the contractor Monday morning and one with the decorator on Wednesday. I'll keep you posted—full report. Oh, and we're going to go ahead and finish a couple of apartments and lofts on the upper floors," he added as Michael started the engine.

Michael turned it back off. "You know we can't afford that."

"They're not hotel rooms, just general living space. All we have to do is paint some walls and install new floors."

"And rewire and plumb."

"Code's going to require us to rewire the whole building anyway. This way, if we do one on each floor, we can use 'em like model homes to lease the rest. Living downtown is hip, especially if you're in a historic building. We get one of those fancy plaques and we're golden. The McMillans on the cutting edge, yet again."

"And if it doesn't work?"

Brady grinned. "I've always dreamed of being a slumlord. Now get out of my hair and go watch SpongeBob."

Michael started the engine. "Okay, but keep me posted on everything."

"From my lips to your ears," Brady promised.

THERE WAS SOMETHING reassuring about airports, Thea thought as she watched Robyn check in for her flight to Australia. Everything was always reassuringly nice and tidy. Arrivals. Departures. You knew whether you were coming or going. It was either one or the other, none of these pesky gray areas.

Like the way she felt about Brady McMillan.

There, she definitely didn't know whether she was coming or going. Sure, she wanted him. Whether it was smart was a whole different topic. And she was supposed to be smart this time around. What she wasn't supposed to do was fall right back into her classic pattern of ignoring all the warning signs and letting chemistry carry the day. That was the perfect recipe for barging into another involvement—however short—that was likely to end badly.

She was hoping that she'd finally learned her lesson.

"There you are, ma'am." The ticket agent handed the folder to Robyn, who slung her backpack over her shoulder. "Have a wonderful trip."

Thea looked at her friend. "All set?"

Most people going on a long-planned vacation looked excited. Robyn looked panicked. "I've forgotten something, I know it."

The corners of Thea's mouth twitched. "You packed three times."

"I still forgot something."

With an indulgent sigh, Thea began ticking things off. "Sunglasses?"

"Check."

"Hotel vouchers?"

"Check."

"Itinerary?"

"Check."

"Moolah?"

Robyn patted her waist.

"Going away present?" Thea produced a brightly wrapped box out of her shoulder bag.

"Go—" Robyn blinked. "You didn't."

"I couldn't resist." Thea handed it to her.

"Aw." Robyn gave her a hug. "You didn't have to do that."

"Open it."

Robyn dropped to a seat in a row of chairs and concentrated on the package. "You're the best, you know. I love you to death, and not because you buy me presents. I love you because you…" She stared at the box in her hand.

"Condoms? You got me condoms as a going away present?" She threw back her head and laughed so loudly a passing group of tourists stared.

"Economy size. A good Girl Scout is always prepared."

"You must think I'm going to need to be prepared a lot." Robyn unzipped her pack and muscled the box inside. "What is that, anyway, the hundred pack?"

"Australia's a big country," Thea said serenely.

"Big men, too. I hope you got extra large."

"I believe there's a variety."

Laughing, they rose to walk toward security. "So come on. I'm there to see the country, and with my cousin, for heaven's sakes. You think I'm going to cut a swath through the men Down Under?"

"I think the men Down Under won't know what hit them. I'm thinking about contacting the Australian embassy."

"Too late." Robyn's voice was triumphant. "It's Friday. By the time they find out, I'll already be in the country. And then, watch out, Bruce." She stopped in the entry area for the security checkpoint and sobered. "Have I told you lately how much I appreciate you coming up?"

"About a million times. Just don't go offering me your firstborn child again. I'm not even sure I want my firstborn child."

"Living with Darlene for three weeks will be good training for you," Robyn advised. "Take care of her, will you?"

"Absolutely. I'll walk her every day, watch soaps with her. We can sit around and do our nails."

Robyn relaxed. "Seriously, though, there's no way I could have gone on this trip if you hadn't shown up. You bailed me out big-time."

"So? You bailed me out last time. It's my turn." And

nothing she could do would ever be enough to pay Robyn back. "Everything's going to be fine, so go on your vacation and don't worry. Whatever you forget, you can buy."

Robyn checked her ticket and passport again. "Now you have the notes and everything, right?"

"I've got the notes and the class lists and everyone's contact info," Thea said crisply, because she could hear the panic returning. "The computer calendar will prompt me on the newsletters."

"And I showed you where to find them?"

"Incessantly. And I know how to send and you've printed out all the details in case the computer goes south. I've got the Moonlight and Tango information and all the information for the tango society. Everything's set. Go." She pushed her toward the TSA officer. "Go on your trip and have fun."

"And the McMillan project." Robyn hopped a few steps and finally gave up and walked. "It's huge. I can't afford to miss on this one. We've got to give them whatever they need."

Thea knew exactly what Brady would decide he needed, and she had no intention of giving it to him. "Everything's going to be fine."

"I know you don't want to deal with him."

"I'm a big girl."

"But you've got to admit, he's cute."

"I'm also a *smart* girl."

"But he seems like a good guy, Thea."

"So did Derek." And like Derek, Brady had a hard time taking no for an answer. Been there, done that, she thought. "All right, enough. Go on your vacation," she ordered. "I'll look after things."

"Promise you'll be nice to him?"

"I'll be nice to him," Thea muttered.

"I mean it, Thea. Swear?"

She relented. "I swear. Trust me, I'll make the McMillan brothers happy."

"Well, there's happy and there's happy. Don't do anything I wouldn't do." Robyn handed her ticket and passport to the security person. "And if you do—" Robyn reached out her hand to Thea, who caught it and discovered she was holding one of the condoms. "Be prepared," Robyn finished with a wicked grin.

Thea gave her a dirty look. "I hope you get savaged by a koala bear."

7

EVERY CITY HAD ITS CLAIM to fame. L.A. had Hollywood, New Orleans had jazz and Portland had rain. Not that Thea had seen much of it so far, with the string of sunny June days. She was seeing the fruits of it now, though—or fruit and vegetables, to be more precise. They were stacked in crates, piled in baskets, arrayed on tables or even heaped in wheelbarrows. They were everywhere she looked in the cornucopia that was the Portland Farmers' Market.

Color leapt out at her: the almost unnatural green of fresh pea tendrils, the luminescent orange of peppers, the inviting blush of peaches. Her mouth watered and she found herself hit by her usual impulse to buy everything in sight.

What was it, anyway, about vegetables that made her feel healthier just by the mere act of buying them? That particular delusion had led her down the garden path—literally—more than once. The result? A crisper full of rotting vegetables. Some, she would eat. Five meals a day, eight days a week? Probably not.

So she cruised the rows instead, feasting with her eyes and enjoying the noise and confusion. So different than L.A. There was something about L.A. that isolated a person, her included. Oh, she had friends, sure, but no real community.

There was something about Portland that brought people together, in the markets, in the coffeehouses, in the parks. And particularly now, she felt a giddiness in the air. In L.A., a sunny day didn't mean much of anything. In Portland, summer was cause for celebration.

Beside her, on the leash, Darlene snuffled, staring around with furrowed brow. "Yeah, I know, you'd be happier if it was a meat market but I can't do anything about that. It's your choice to be a carnivore," Thea told her.

Darlene just made an impatient noise.

Thea stopped at a booth selling strawberries. "Two dollars," said the woman behind the table. "Twenty-two for the flat. They're Chandlers, picked this morning."

They didn't have the bizarre, distorted shape of grocery store strawberries. These were like centerfold strawberries, full, succulent, gleaming red and perfectly shaped. The aroma alone was enough to make her almost dizzy. They looked almost too perfect to be true, she thought, picking up a berry to study the glossy ruby skin, the even dips, the careful speckle of seeds. She could already taste the burst of sweetness as she bit down into it.

"Go ahead," a voice said in her ear. "You know you want to."

Thea jumped, dropped the berry back into the basket.

And turned to find Brady McMillan, directly behind her. He grinned, his teeth very white in the morning sun. "The tango lady, right?"

Thea took a breath, waiting for her system to level out from the fright. Of course, this was Brady, so expecting it to level might be entirely too much. She gave him a narrow-eyed look. "That was an evil thing to do."

"Sorry," he said unrepentantly. "I didn't realize you were such a strawberry fan."

Why was it every time she turned around, he was there? It would all be so much easier if he didn't set butterflies loose in her stomach, Thea thought, staring up into those amused green eyes. He wore khaki shorts and a navy T-shirt that read If You Tap It, They Will Come. His hair looked as though he hadn't bothered to do much more than run his fingers through it; the shadow on his chin suggested that he hadn't bothered shaving, either. She doubted that he'd thought more than two minutes about how he looked when he'd left the house.

How was it he still looked sexy as hell?

Down, girl.

It was that coming-and-going thing again—half of her wanted nothing more than the coming part, preferably literally. The other half knew the intelligent thing to do would be to get away from him as fast as she could.

If only.

Promise me you'll be nice. Robyn's business, she reminded herself. She owed Robyn, and if that meant making nice with Brady McMillan for a few minutes, she would.

"So who's this?" he asked, crouching down to rub Darlene's neck as she wriggled deliriously.

"It's Darlene, Robyn's pug."

"Darlene?" He chuckled.

Darlene swiveled her head as though it were on a pivot, staring at him with her pop-eyes. Thea swore her jaw jutted out even farther. "I wouldn't make fun of her name, if I were you," she said mildly. "She might look small, but I bet she could take you."

Brady studied Darlene's furrowed brow. "I bet she could, too." He rubbed her ears some more. "I'll watch my step."

Darlene looked mollified and leaned hard against his hand.

"So why don't you have a dog? You seem like a dog guy."

He shrugged. "I am. I did. Spike, a border collie. He died a couple months back."

He kept his voice light, but she saw the flicker in his eyes as he rose. "I'm sorry."

"Yeah, me too. It's funny the habits you get into," he said. "I keep going out to the Jeep and finding myself looking around, thinking he'll be jumping into the back."

"Maybe you should get another one."

He studied her. "I will. I wanted to let a few months go by first."

His eyes were that deep green, like looking into the reflection of a forest in a mountain pool. And then she felt like she was falling into it, tipping somehow deeper than she'd ever imagined, until it filled up her world.

Thea shook her head abruptly, resurfacing with a blink. Suddenly awkward, she moved on down the aisle. Brady began to walk with her.

He drifted to a stop at a stand selling raspberries and blueberries. "So what are the chances of us running into each other here?"

"You took the words right out of my mouth."

He smiled. "Relax. I'm not stalking you. Portland can be a small town sometimes." He inspected the berries in one flat, then the next.

Thea eyed him. "Really? I wouldn't have picked you to be a big veggie guy."

"I'm a big fan of food in general," he said easily, handing some bills to the vendor. "But right now, I'm working on a project." He winked and hoisted a flat of raspberries. "Raw materials."

He didn't look like much of a chef and curiosity got the best of her. "Planning to cook?"

"Not cook, brew."

"With raspberries." She moved out of the way for a couple with their stroller.

He gave her a sunny smile. "Yep."

"Raspberry beer?"

"Raspberry ale. It's that pushing-the-envelope thing."

"Anybody ever tell you that your envelope might not be quite squared off?"

His mouth curved. "Now you're giving me compliments."

"That wasn't a compliment." She stopped to pick out some wax beans and he stopped with her.

"Sure it was. Regular is boring. I'd rather do something different."

"Like raspberry beer."

"Ale," he corrected. "I have to follow my muse."

She glanced at him, well over six feet tall, tanned and built, his bicep swelling slightly as he held the berries up on his shoulder. "Your muse?"

"I do what the beer needs." He watched her pick through some patty pan squash. "What are those?"

"Flying saucers," she told him.

"They look more like throwing stars. I can see it now, murder by produce. No wonder your friend Robyn went off to Australia. She did go, right?"

Thea paid for the squash and added it to her bag. "Last night. Right now, she's probably on about hour seventeen of being crammed into an airplane and ready to scream."

Brady shook his head. "Nope, no way. I'd never make it. I'd go flat out nuts."

"Don't like being cooped up?"

"I'm not what you call sized for planes. Besides, I like being outdoors. You know, fresh air, sun?"

"Or rain, if you live here."

"Hey, if I'm kayaking, I'm wet anyway. And if I'm hiking, I can wear a jacket. You hike?" he asked, skirting a display of melons.

"Not so much. I mostly bike."

"We should go for a ride sometime while you're here. Ride to Brimfield—that's one of our hotel pubs. It's right outside the city. I bet you'd like it."

"Speaking of Brimfield, I'm still not getting why you're here. I thought you guys grow all your own produce out there. And at the school. What are you doing buying stuff here?"

His lips twitched. "Way to change the subject. Flawless."

"Thanks. I've been practicing."

"Hard work pays off."

Around him, it was a survival skill.

"So, you been studying up on us?"

"Robyn told me," she muttered, concentrating fiercely on a display of dazzlingly ripe tomatoes. "Don't get all excited. It's just business."

"Crushed, yet again. I can hold your dog while you're picking those out," he added, and took the leash to control Darlene, who was tugging madly to get over and sniff a passing black lab. "Anyway, I'd love to get the goods from the gardens. The problem is, the chefs all seem to think that they should have priority."

"Like food is more important than beer," Thea said in mock outrage.

"Exactly. I could arm wrestle them for it," he reflected, "but I wouldn't want to hurt them. Besides, if I come here, I get free food."

"Free food?"

"Sure." He gave her Darlene's leash back as they started

walking again. "Haven't you ever been here before? The food's the best part. They give out free samples, at least as long as you've bought something. Come on, I'll show you."

THE COOKING DEMONSTRATIONS always seemed to get the biggest crowds, but as far as Brady was concerned, they only counted if you got to eat the results. He led Thea down the row toward the food area. Pea tendrils today in the chef's tent, he saw. Somehow, it wasn't making his mouth water.

"Look how pretty," Thea said.

"There's better to be had, I'm betting." He kept going, following a savory scent that was coming on the breeze. Ahead, a pony-tailed guy with the stringy look of a committed vegetarian tended to a grill. On the table beside him sat rondelles of roasted corn with skewers poked in them.

"Wow, that smells great," Thea said.

She'd relaxed, he realized. Maybe it was the walking and talking, maybe it was her foolish little dog, but she seemed at ease. Good that one of them was, because he hadn't been able to stop thinking about touching her since they'd met. She wore a purple shirt over grayish athletic shorts that showed a lot of those long, luscious legs of hers. Her throat looked soft and smooth.

She had her hair skinned back from her face in a hair band. She didn't even have on lipstick, so why was it he couldn't stop watching her mouth? And her eyes, those soft blue-gray eyes, sparkling with interest. He was happy he could show her something that made her look like that. He wanted her to look that way at him.

Patience, he reminded himself.

Preferably immediately. Though, he wanted a lot of things immediately just then.

"Oh good grief they've got blueberry shortcake," Thea breathed. "I may just have died and gone to heaven."

"Does that mean I have to watch your dog?"

"Would you?" She looped the leash over his wrist. "I'm just going to the shortcake table. It's a shorter trip than heaven." She stopped. "Do you want some?"

"I never turn down sweet things."

He let himself watch her walk away for a minute, then lowered the flat of berries to sling them under one arm. "What do you think, Darlene, is she going to give us some?"

Darlene frowned up at him as though he were some zoo exhibit, ratcheting her head around on her neck to get a better look.

Thea hurried over. "Got it," she said triumphantly, holding up the two bowls.

Brady glanced from the flat of raspberries he held to Darlene's leash. "Yeah, I'm sort of manually challenged right now."

"Let me take her back."

"I'll need more than that. Why don't you have yours, then we'll trade?"

"You shouldn't have to wait," she objected.

"I don't mind." And he didn't; after all, he'd get to watch.

"Just a couple of bites," she bargained, clearly uncomfortable at the idea of eating when he wasn't.

It made him smile. "You did all the work, you get first taste," he said. "You're allowed." Encouraged, would be more like it, he thought as he watched her spoon up a bite of the shortcake and slip it into her mouth.

She closed her eyes for an instant and he felt a surge of warmth at the pleasure on her face. She gave herself over to it in the same way she'd given herself over to orgasm when they'd been in bed that one night. That one night that had damned well better turn into more. Just remembering had the warmth turning into heat.

Thea hummed. "This is incredible."

Her lips were what was incredible, he thought feverishly as she took another bite. He watched them close around the spoon, unable to keep from watching as she savored the taste with that same abandonment.

"You've got to try this," she said, stepping toward him. "Here, just taste this."

Brady leaned in. He meant to take the bite, so help him he did. But she'd left a bit of whipped cream on her upper lip and he found himself watching it, staring as she came closer. Suddenly he didn't give a damn about the dessert, all he wanted was her mouth. And then he was tasting her, tasting the cream, the sweetness of berries, the sweetness that was all her, feeling the soft exhalation of her breath, hearing the plop as the shortcake hit the ground.

And he didn't give a damn about that and he didn't give a damn about the people passing by or the dog at their feet because she was kissing him back, her mouth warm and soft and mobile. Then she stepped into him and slid her hand around his neck and it was all he could do to hold onto the fool raspberries. He cursed the fact that he'd ever bought them because all he wanted was to bring her against him, to feel that long, strong body. Only being able to touch her with his mouth was torture.

Time was elastic, immaterial. Brady didn't know how long it had been. It didn't matter. All that mattered was more.

But they were in public and the berries were his salvation. They reminded him that there was an outside world, they kept him from going too far. Even so, when he dragged himself back, he was almost dizzied with it. He moved back because he wanted to take this somewhere private and quiet where there would be no interruptions.

Thea's eyes looked as stunned as he felt. She stared at him blankly, touched the back of her hand to her mouth, then glanced down to where Darlene was busy licking the last bits of shortcake. "I should go," she said faintly,

"We should go," he corrected, reaching for her arm.

"No." She picked up the trash and tossed it in a nearby bin, then took Darlene's leash. "I have things to get done."

Stifling impatience, he followed her as she walked toward the parking area. "When am I going to see you again?"

"Leave a message at the studio."

"I'm not talking about work."

"I am." She stopped and turned to face him. "While Robyn's gone, I'm handling her part of the project for you."

"So?"

"So that's business. And we…this other stuff doesn't fit with business." She turned and began to walk again.

"Why not?" He gave her a sidelong glance. "Don't you trust yourself not to molest me on the job site? Not that I'd complain."

"Be serious."

"Not my specialty."

"If we're working together, we don't need to get anything started between us."

He felt frustration again. "Oh, come on. It's going already and you know it."

"And it's stopping right now."

"Why? What's the problem? Because it sure isn't anything you've talked about." And if he didn't know what he was up against, how could he fight it?

She let out an anxious breath. "Look, this project is really important, to Robyn—and to you, I assume. I don't think we should mix business and..."

"And?"

She moved her head. "Sex," she said finally. She stopped before a blue Prius and shook out her keys.

"I don't see what one has to do with the other. It's not like we work for some big company where anyone would care. We're adults. Work's work and personal stuff is personal stuff. We ought to be able to keep them separate."

"You can't possibly be that naive." She put her bags in the trunk.

"And you're overcomplicating things." He set the flat of berries on the roof. "And don't tell me this is about the tango theater because you were running away way before that."

Something flared in her eyes. "I'm not running away."

"What do you call it, then?" he demanded. "You kissed me back there. What was that all about? Blueberry shortcake?"

"It was a mistake."

"You seem to have a habit of making them when we're together," he said tightly. "Doesn't that tell you something?"

"Yes. It tells me we should stay away from each other."

"Dammit, what do I have to do, start scheduling lessons to get time with you? Because I'll do it."

Thea let Darlene onto the driver's seat and shifted to face him. "This is exactly what I'm talking about. You're already blurring the lines."

"Well, as long as I'm blurring," he told her, stepping forward. And dragged her to him.

Like the fumes swirling in the instant before spontaneous combustion, the annoyance and impatience and desire formed a potent mix that burst into pure heat. Brady dove into the kiss, ravaging her mouth, that wide, soft mobile mouth that kept him awake at night, staring at the ceiling. Now it was against his, avid and greedy because she was kissing him back, matching him move for move, igniting that desperate craving. Need drummed through him, desperation gripped him.

Brady knew it was too hard, too aggressive but he was powerless to stop himself. He'd thought of her, imagined her, ached for her. And now she was here, in his arms.

It was amazing, incredible, outrageous.

It wasn't even close to enough.

THEA FELT HIS LIPS CRUSH down on hers as though he were branding her, burning every thought from her mind but the need for more. The taste of him sent her reeling. The feel of his body against hers only made her want. His hands were hard on her hips, her ass, her breasts, marking her as his even as she slid her arms around his back. For balance, she could tell herself, but it was a lie. She just wanted. She wanted to taste, she wanted to touch. She wanted him naked.

She wanted everything.

She'd had all-night sex with him, she'd kissed him only minutes before. Kissing him now shouldn't have sent desire thundering through her until she couldn't think straight, couldn't think about anything except tasting him, being against him, having him. It made her giddy. It exhilarated her.

It terrified her.

In the car, Darlene gave an impatient yip.

Brady raised his head, breathing hard. Staring at Thea, obviously waiting to see what she would say.

If he only knew. Thea pushed away, wishing her pulse would slow down. Arrivals. Departures. Coming and going. Wanting. Ultimately, it all came down to the wanting, and she didn't know what to do about it. But she needed to sort it out and sort it out soon before she drove both of them crazy.

Brady stayed silent, eyes watchful.

Thea licked her lips. "Things are complicated right now," she began.

"Are you involved with someone? Is that the problem?"

She shook her head. How could she tell him that the involvement had ended eight years before, but that it was only now reaching the end in her mind? "Look, I know I seem like a flake and that I'm jerking you around. I'm sorry. I don't mean to be. I have stuff I need to work through. And I don't know how I'm going to do that or when. The smartest thing you could do is write me off."

"I don't know how smart that would be. And I'm not sure that's what either one of us wants me to do, really. I think I'd rather stick around, see how it all turns out."

"It might not," she warned him.

He tucked a strand of hair behind her ear. "I'm willing to take my chances." When she opened her mouth to speak, he brushed a quick kiss over her lips then picked up his berries. "Excuse me, I've got some beer to brew."

8

IT WAS AMAZING what a difference a few days could make, Brady thought as he walked into the Odeon theater lobby. Or what was left of it. The carpet was long gone, ditto for the wallpaper. Nearby, a team of electricians were busy stripping out old conduit in preparation for rewiring the building. The interior of the theater was stripped to its elegant bones and the reconstructive surgery had begun.

The old lobby candy counter had been taken out and pushed to one side. It would stay; they'd use it to sell T-shirts, hats, promo merchandise for any of the live shows they chose to have. To the other side, behind panes of glass, would be the microbrewery. He'd already bought the equipment; it was a matter of reinforcing the floors so that it could be installed.

The pounding of hammers and the scything growl of chainsaws echoed through the auditorium as Brady stepped to the doorway. It was taking shape before his eyes. The motley old seats were history, yanked out and tossed into the Dumpster that sat out on the curb. In their place rose the support structure of what would be the terraced restaurant. The lounge would be in the seats on the second level; at the back on both floors would be polished dark walnut bars with direct lines down to the basement cold room. The effect would be equal parts opulence and nostalgia, guests equally comfortable in suits or jeans.

It was coming together, he thought in satisfaction.

And then he stopped. Walking up the side of the auditorium toward him was Michael. Brady narrowed his eyes a fraction and watched his brother busily talking on his cell phone. Michael finished the call and stepped through the doorway to the lobby. Casually, Brady shifted to one side.

"Looking for tools to fix your baby crib?"

Michael's head snapped around to stare at him. "Brady. You're here early."

Brady nodded. "Every day. I could say the same for you."

Michael coughed. "Had to go out to get some groceries."

"At seven in the morning?"

"Gave me time to stop by and see how things are going."

Relax, Brady told himself. It was nothing more than what it looked like.

So why did he feel like Michael was checking up on him?

He shook it off. "Didn't I say I'd give you a full rundown?"

Michael made a show of studying the candy counter. "I thought I'd save you the trouble."

"Well, let's go touch base with Hal, see how things are going."

"I already did."

This time, the twinge of exasperation was definite. "Did we pass inspection?"

"Hal says there's a problem with the plumbing. It looks pretty extensive but I can't stick around right now to help figure out what to do." He checked his watch. "Lindsay's got a doctor's appointment. I won't be done until around eleven."

He'd asked Hal to wait until he could come back, Brady

realized. Calm, he thought. Keep it calm. "Then it's a good thing I'm here, isn't it? I'll take care of it."

"I might be able to come back—"

"I said I'd take care of it." The calm slipped a notch before he got it back. "Trust me, Michael," Brady enunciated. "You're going to have to."

"Of course I trust you," Michael said a little too quickly. "It's just that we've got a lot of money tied up in this."

"You think I'm not aware of that?"

They locked gazes, green against brown. The seconds ticked by. Finally Michael let out a breath. "All right. I'll leave you to it, then."

Brady stood with his hands on his hips, staring across the lobby after Michael, staring into the auditorium. Down by the stage Hal, the contractor, raised his hand. Consciously relaxing, Brady headed toward him.

"Morning, Hal."

"Morning." Silver-haired and sun-browned, Hal Worley had an air of quiet authority that suggested nothing short of world apocalypse—and perhaps not even that—would rattle him. If a natural disaster hit, Hal would blink, open up his binder and pull out his contingency plan. He'd been the contractor on each of the other four pub renovations and Brady was heartily glad to have him.

Hal straightened up from studying plans spread out on a table formed of a plywood sheet laid over sawhorses.

"I hear there's something going on with the plumbing," Brady said. And it bugged him that he hadn't found out first.

Hal shrugged. "We've got a surprise or two. Sort of goes with the territory in a building this old."

"They're not surprises, Hal, they're idiosyncrasies."

"Hmm, we've got ourselves some pretty damned idio-syncratic plumbing in the dressing rooms. On the first checks I found copper, but it's spliced in with brass, alu-minum and I don't know what all else."

Ka-ching. "How bad?"

"That's just it. Most of it's fine but a couple of parts are corroded and some of the rest is ready to go. We can fix the problems, or while you've got everything split open we can do the whole thing. Cost you more up front but you'll save money in the long term."

"How long term?"

Hal shrugged. "Could go next week, next year, could last another ten or twenty. If budget and schedule didn't matter, I'd say rip it all out and put in new, but of course…"

Funny how nothing about a project quite went accord-ing to plan, Brady thought. "Got estimates?"

"Right here." Hal pulled a sheet out of his binder. "Mi-chael said he'd come back—"

"Michael won't be back today. It's on my plate."

Brady considered the figures, mentally comparing them to the slush fund he'd left in the budget. Pay me now, pay me later—the question was which.

"Want to go take a look at it?" Hal asked.

Carpentry, Brady knew. And tile and even some wiring. He'd done enough projects with friends and family and work on his house that he had experience. Plumbing, though, he knew eff-all about plumbing.

He had a sudden feeling he'd better learn, and quickly.

"You should also know about the stage." Hal put down his pencil.

Great. More idiosyncrasies. "What about the stage?"

"I'd planned to buff it down and refinish it but the grain

keeps coming up. It's in worse shape than I originally thought and there's some delamination in the subflooring. We can go ahead with the plan, but it's not going to be really smooth and flat. Do you care? If you want a sprung wood surface, it's not going to be cheap. I'll need to know about it soon."

If he answered, he'd be guessing. They weren't going to be hosting ballet troupes and the outdoor tango dance had been on concrete. Brady considered. "How soon?"

"No later than Friday. Tomorrow morning would be better—I've got to go to the building supply."

Brady pulled out his cell phone and started to dial the digits of the studio phone number that he'd already committed to memory. No hardship having a reason to call Thea. Then again, why do by phone what was best done in person? A slow smile spread over his face and he pressed the button to end the call.

"Let's take a look at that plumbing," he told Hal. "I'll get back to you on the stage question by tomorrow."

A LOBOTOMY MIGHT be the answer, Thea thought as she watched her class walk through a new rumba figure. Okay, granted there was the loss of I.Q. and personality and, well, virtually everything else, but at least it would give her a rest from thinking about Brady McMillan. In junior high school, yes, it had been okay to spend her every waking hour thinking about a boy. In high school, even. By now, though, she ought to have been long past replaying conversations over and over in her mind, past getting butterflies when she thought of a man's kisses.

But what kisses.

"Okay, I see some of you are missing the step-brush-step after the pivot. Let's run through it again." She glanced behind herself to ensure that the ranks of students were following suit and began to talk them through the step.

It was a miracle that she was managing to teach at all. Robyn certainly had a right to expect better, and if Thea could decide what to do about Brady, she could offer it. The problem was, it was too complicated. There was what she thought she ought to want and what she really wanted. Every other time she'd gone with what she'd wanted, it had been a disaster, starting with her high school boyfriend. Who was to say that things with Brady would be any different?

And yet how would she ever know without trying?

"On the five step walkaround, don't forget the arm movements. Serve up the imaginary glass of water on a tray as your hand goes away, then dump it out as you curve your hand back toward yourself."

Of course, you could get yourself hurt while trying if you weren't careful. If you didn't keep control. The problem was she didn't know if that was possible. Just remembering that kiss in the parking lot made her shiver a little. Just thinking about his taste sent that sweet ache through her. Days had passed since the farmers' market and she still had no better idea of what she wanted to do. Days had passed and still she fell asleep thinking about him, she woke up thinking about him. He was on her mind when she was in the shower, eating dinner, getting dressed, getting undressed—especially undressed—and, of course, at work.

"Okay, let's go through it one last time together and call it a night. Joe?"

Thea held out her hand to her volunteer teaching assistant. The slow pulse of the music began and Joe led her into the step.

Yes, especially at work, every time she was in the back studio, before the mirrors. She pivoted out and moved into the walkaround. Every time she heard the music of the tango. Every time she looked to the front of the studio, to the barrier where she'd seen him standing, elbows folded on the counter.

She served her imaginary water glass up, poured it out as she came around.

And as though she'd conjured him by thinking, he was there, arms folded on the counter, watching her.

She froze.

He grinned at her, looking relaxed and comfortable. Looking good enough to eat.

"You okay?" asked Joe.

She'd stopped in her tracks, Thea realized. She gave herself a mental shake. "Oh, sure, yeah. Okay," she raised her voice to the class, "that about wraps it up for tonight. I'll see you next week, same bat time, same bat channel."

There was the usual hubbub of a group of people all heading off the floor at the same time, hurrying to change shoes, get out into the summer evening. Thea took her time, fielding questions, shutting off the lights in the back studio, closing the windows.

Trying to figure out what to say to him.

Trying to figure out what she wanted.

Finally, she shut off the stereo and walked over to where Brady stood, watching her. "Nice dress," he commented.

"Thanks." It was vivid blue, short and flippy. Not one of her usual somber shades but somehow she'd lost her taste for black and charcoal in the succession of golden summer days. "What brings you around?"

"I wanted to tap my resident tango expert."

"You did happen to notice we're closed, right?" She came through the gap in the barrier, giving him wide berth.

"Good. I guess that means that you're through for the night." He followed her over to Robyn's office, leaning against the doorway to watch as she dug out her keys and the small shoulder bag she used for a purse, his gaze making her exaggeratedly aware of her movements.

The answering machine light was blinking and she pressed the button. With a beep, Robyn's voice vaulted out into the room. "Thea, hey, I was hoping to catch you before the last class. Just checking in to see how everything's going. I hope you're having fun because I have to warn you, I may never be coming home. I swear, you've never seen men this gorgeous. I've been working my way through your going-away present so fast I may run out. Anyway, I hope everything's fine. You know where to reach me if you need anything. Oh, and don't forget to be nice to Brady McMillan. But don't do anything I wouldn't do," she cackled. "Love you, honey. Bye."

There was a click and the message ended.

Brady looked amused. "Going-away present?"

"Nothing," Thea muttered, cheeks heating as she walked past him into the entry area. "Look, can we talk tomorrow? It's the end of the day and I'm tired." And not up to dealing with emotions.

"How about dinner?"

"How about not?" She locked the office.

"You said you're tired. All the more reason you should let someone else do the cooking. Besides, Robyn told you to be nice to me."

She glowered at him. "What's this about?"

"A blatant attempt to soften you up so you'll let me drag

you by the theater to answer some tango-related construction questions that I don't have a clue about."

"Does it have to be tonight?" She started down the stairs to the front door.

"So says Hal the contractor, who's going to be at Portland Lumber and Building Supply ordering materials tomorrow morning." Brady followed on her heels. "Now, you could say no, but that means he'll have to hold off, which could slow down construction, which'll delay the opening of the theater, which'll cost us more money, possibly bankrupting us and forcing my brother to sell his soon-to-be-born twins into the white slave trade."

Thea stopped with her hand on the door to the outside and turned to him. "The white slave trade, huh?"

"It'll be on your conscience."

"So why not go to the theater now?"

"Because I'm starving. Besides, I know this great brewpub that makes the best fries in town. And the beer's pretty good, too."

Thea crossed her arms and stared at him. "The brewmaster's name wouldn't start with an *M* by any chance, would it?" she asked.

"A name you can trust. Anyway, I've got the keys to the theater. We can swing by any time. No reason we can't go out first."

"We're not going out," she warned herself as much as him.

He opened the door for her. "Of course we're not."

HE WAS RIGHT, Thea thought, they were about the best fries she'd ever tasted. And yes, the beer was pretty good, too. She didn't know if it was the hops or the fact that the little glasses of the tasting flight added up, but she was actually relaxing.

Around Brady, that was a first.

She'd worked her way through the tasting and settled on the summer ale. It was light, crisp, with a hint of something she couldn't quite identify. She drank some and frowned.

"What?" Brady asked.

"This has got lemon in it, right? And…" She took another sip. "Rosemary?"

He beamed at her. "Good palate. Most people don't even notice it over the hops. We'll make you a brewmaster yet."

"Don't I have to know how to make beer, first?"

"A good palate is the most important requirement. Makes you try beer and think about what you really wish you were drinking."

"What got you started?" She felt the warm mellowness spread through her.

Brady grinned. "I liked drinking it and I ran out one night."

"Seriously."

"Seriously? I don't know, I wanted to figure it out, I guess. It seemed kind of like magic. You mix water and hops and malt into this god-awful-looking mess, and somehow out of that you get something like this." He held his glass up to the light, where it shone clear and gold.

"Is that what you like about it, the magic?"

"I like that I get to use both parts of my brain. It's part art, part science. There's stuff I can quantify and get exact and there's other stuff that's just—" he moved his shoulders "—instinct, I guess."

She'd never thought of it like that. "You don't have standard recipes?"

"It's kind of like being a chef. There's the basic stuff and then you jump off from there. That's what I like—I get an idea, I can try it. And taste the results in two weeks," he added.

"Like raspberry ale?"

"Like raspberry ale." Up at the front, a group of thirty-somethings sang a round of "Happy Birthday" and raised their glasses in a toast. Brady's eyes met hers. "I also like seeing people enjoy themselves." He shrugged. "It's not the cure for cancer but it's what I do."

And, endearingly, he looked suddenly bashful.

The warmth she felt was just the beer, Thea told herself. "How do you learn a job like this? I mean, how long have you been doing it?" she asked, to keep her mind occupied.

"Since I was a sophomore in college. Ninety-five. That's what, twelve years?"

Which made him two years older than she was, she realized. And then thought again. "Twenty? But that's…"

"Yep. But it wasn't like I was buying alcohol. I was just buying malt and hops and yeast. Harmless."

Thea coughed. "Good luck with that one. You ever try it out on the cops?"

He gave her a broad grin. "Never had a reason to. I don't think I made anything worth drinking anyway until I was twenty-one."

"I take it it's not as easy as following the recipe. How was your first batch?"

"Stunk to high heaven," he said cheerfully. "So did the next five or six. Too much carbonation, not enough fermentation, bacteria in the fermenting tank, you name it. I'd have given up but I've got what you call a stubborn streak."

"You didn't brew it here, did you?"

"Oh, hell no. At home, or my dorm room, actually."

"Your dorm room?"

His eyes twinkled. "I had supportive roommates."

"So how did you go from brewing in your dorm room to this?" she waved at the copper tanks.

"Michael was managing the restaurant that was here around the time I graduated. He liked the work and I liked brewing, and Oregon had just passed legislation that opened the door for brewpubs. So we worked two jobs apiece, pooled our money. When the owners of his restaurant decided to sell, we figured that was our opening. Once we got enough ahead to pop for the brewing equipment, we brought in a brewmaster and started rolling."

Thea took a swallow of the summer ale. "And let me guess, you laid for the guy one night, knocked him off and took his job."

"Close. He got snapped up by a microbrewery up in Seattle about two years after he came on board. By that time, I'd been brewing for four years and working under him for two. Michael was willing to give me a chance. I worked my butt off and everything came together. Come on." He rose. "I'll give you a tour."

Worts and mash, malts and hops. Mash tun and brew kettle and fermenter. The process was a fascinating blur of precision and by guess and by golly. Art and science, indeed. For every one of her questions Brady addressed with a concrete answer, there were three or four more that came down to a brewer's experience.

He walked her through the tanks looking for all the world like a proud homeowner, talking offhandedly about a process in which an error could cause five hundred gallons of product to be dumped—and leave the taps dry. He said he didn't do serious, but the line of plaques hung up on the wall testified to the fact that he was seriously good at what he did.

And dedicated.

"You're like one of those circus clowns with the plates on sticks," Thea told him. "You're brewing here, fermenting there, aging there, all at the same time."

"And performing quality control at the end, don't forget. That's my favorite part."

They stood on a metal platform tucked between the hot-tub-sized brew kettle and the equally large mash tun. "And you do this all for four places?"

"Times six beers." He leaned past her to close the hatch on the empty mash tun, the hairs on his forearm brushing hers.

And her thoughts scattered like a flock of startled birds. His work. They'd been talking about his work. "So, um, how do you keep up? You must work constantly."

"It varies. Sometimes it's a few hours, sometimes it's an eighteen hour day. I'm here when the beer needs me."

Her lips twitched. "When the beer needs you?"

"Yep." Suddenly, the fun in his eyes shifted into something else, a heat, an intensity. "Of course, if you were to decide you needed me instead, I might be what you call conflicted."

That quickly, her mouth went dry and the platform seemed very small. It had been easy to relax with him, to forget he was the Brady who could kiss her half blind. He didn't seem so safe and easy anymore.

She moistened her lips. "I'll try to avoid putting you on the spot. So what was all this about the theater?" Going back to business was good. It'd give her a chance to get her brain functioning again, a chance to determine what in the hell she thought she was doing.

"The contractor's got a question about the stage surface. That comes back to dance stuff, and since you're my dance expert, I figured I'd come to you."

"So ask away."

"Well, it might be easier if I took you down and showed you. Are you ready to go, or do I need to ply you with more beer?"

"I think I'm about as plied as I need to be," Thea answered, waving a hand toward the stairs. "Lead the way."

9

OUTSIDE, THE EVENING WAS WARM as they walked to his truck. The theater was the thing. That was what Thea needed to concentrate on, not on this feeling that the ground was shifting under her feet, that what she thought she wanted—keeping her distance from Brady McMillan—was no longer possible.

"So talk to me about your project."

"My project?" Brady echoed. "The beer? Oh, the theater. It's been interesting."

"How so?"

"I'm learning a lot of new stuff."

"Really? This is number what, five? I'd think you guys would have the drill down by now."

"That's just the thing. We've always sort of split the job. I've been involved in the renovations, but not at the center of it all. I'm the beer and idea man—"

"One of those creative types."

"Exactly. And Michael likes to run things."

"Older brother?" she guessed.

He nodded. "Definitely. I'll be seventy-five and he'll be eighty and he'll still be performing the big brother act."

"Sometimes the stuff you grow up with is the hardest in the world to get past." It was something she understood better than most.

"Oh, the split's always worked pretty well before. Michael's been hinting lately that he wants more help, but when it comes down to it, I don't think he can make himself give it up. That mind-body split thing." He gave her a side-long glance. "You'd know about that."

Thea smiled. "Following through on what you know you ought to do isn't always easy," she said as they came to a stop by his Jeep. She leaned against the side of the vehicle. For a moment, Brady just looked at her, his eyes darkened with shadows, but not so much that she couldn't read his intent.

"How's that thinking going?" he asked, bracing his hands against the roof on either side of her and leaning in toward her. "Anything changed?"

"I don't know," she whispered, watching. Waiting. Wanting.

A long second dragged by. Then another.

"Mmm." He stepped back and brought out his keys. "Anyway." He cleared his throat. "Well, the division of labor has worked pretty well and that was how we were planning it this time, too. But things went off the rails last Saturday, as I think you kind of figured out. Now his wife's on bedrest."

"The one pregnant with the twins?"

"Bingo." He opened the door for her and helped her in. "The only way we could do the theater was for me to take it on."

It was only a light touch on her arm. It still raised goose bumps. Now it was her turn to clear her throat. "So Michael got his way?"

Brady shrugged. "I kind of volunteered. I figured it was about time. He needed the help, I wanted the theater."

Thea reached for the door handle. "How's it working out? Interesting, I think you said? Is that like the old curse, 'May you live in interesting times'?"

"Yeah, well, every day should be full of new surprises." He shut the door and came around to the driver's side.

"Leaves less time for kayaking," Thea observed.

"Yeah, but the place is going to be great. We'll maybe have twenty-five, thirty rooms, plus the restaurant and bars. It's got box seats up on the side walls. We're building rooms outside of them so that if you're staying there, the box seats are your balcony."

"Nice. I hope you've got good soundproofing."

"The best. Now if I could decide on the rooms."

"Aren't you the idea man?"

"I am."

"Maybe you need to drink more beer."

"Maybe," he said thoughtfully. "The problem is, we're using the same decorator as we have at the other properties, but this time out of the gate I don't think she gets it. She wants to go with something really stagy—props, backdrops, klieg lights, all that."

"I suppose some of that could work," Thea said doubtfully. "It could be over the top, though. Which is not necessarily a bad thing—"

"Except when it is."

She laughed. "Well, what about going the other way? Do them like dressing rooms. Maybe even move the real dressing rooms somewhere else so that you can make the original dressing rooms into premium suites. You know, stars on the door, the mirrored vanity, the whole nine yards." She laid one hand dramatically against her chest. "'I'm ready for my close-up, now, Mr. DeMille.'"

Brady watched her, considering. "You know, that's not a bad idea. Putting rooms so close to the stage, though, it won't be easy."

"Isn't that what you idea men are all about, challenges?"

"We idea men are about creating challenges for other people."

"Look at it as an opportunity for personal growth. Anyway, it's a thought. So what's your question?"

He started the engine. "I'll show you when we get there."

SHE HADN'T THOUGHT it would be dark. Spacious? Sure. Ornate? Absolutely. She'd expected it to echo, perhaps. She hadn't reckoned with the tomblike blackness.

Brady cursed. "I thought Hal would leave some lights on down front."

"Hal?"

"The contractor. I guess he doesn't trust the wiring. Wait here. I'll get a flashlight."

It was black anodized steel, the size of a small cannon. "You could murder someone with that thing," she pointed out.

"It's safer than a squash. Come on."

Even with the powerful flashlight, the edges of the lobby receded into dimness. "The electricians are rewiring the whole thing. There are still some live outlets down by the stage. You want me to go in and switch them on while you wait?"

"No," she responded immediately. It was silly to send him there as if she was some helpless female who was afraid of the dark. She had on flats, she'd be safe enough.

"Let's go, then," he said. "It's not that far and Hal keeps a good, clean site. Stick with me and you'll be fine."

It was the sticking with him part that worried her.

Brady stretched one arm before her to shine the flashlight. He kept the other lightly touching her back as a guide. "It wasn't too bad when I was in here earlier today, but things can change."

They already had, she realized. Maybe it was the cave-like darkness or maybe it was the quiet that drew the cloak of intimacy around them. They'd become a circle of two. She should have been watching where she was going; instead, she focused on the sound of his breath, the heat from his fingertips against her spine.

"You've got to see this place," he continued. "You're going to love it." His voice sent a little hum through her like a subsonic vibration. And somewhere deep inside her, a low, distant drumbeat of desire began to thud in response.

"Talk to me about the theater," she said somewhat desperately.

"Watch out." He caught her against him. For a moment, all she could feel was the heat of his body. "You almost walked into that pile of two-by-fours."

He released her and her heart, after a pause, started beating again.

"The theater? It's pretty incredible. Built in the thirties, when they really knew how to do it. For burlesque, at first, then movies. It went downhill in the sixties and seventies, though. Turned into a porn theater by the end."

She thought of Paige's stories of the burlesque museum, the costumes, the sexuality. That was it, she thought feverishly. It was the leftover vibe of all those decades. It was the heat and immediacy of walking so close together. It was her years of deprivation. It sure as hell was something because all the good reasons in the world had become meaningless.

She wanted him and she couldn't stop.

"The back half will be a raised bar and restaurant, but the front will still have those red velvet seats that look like they belong in a brothel. And we'll have you, dancing tango onstage. I'm thinking they'll come," he added. "They'll definitely come."

They'll come.

They were closer to the stage, now. She had an impression of a shadowy bulk, then saw the raised platform appear in the beam. She swallowed. "So what was your question?"

"It's about the stage surface. The contractor thinks it might be too rough. I want your opinion."

"Let's get up there, then."

They stopped before the stage. "The steps are blocked right now, sorry," he said. "We have other ways, though." He set the flashlight up on end, so that it threw a cone of light that faded off into the darkness above. The glow spread over their faces and faintly lit the stage for a few feet.

When he put his hands on her waist, he caught her by surprise. She gave a yelp and clutched his shoulders out of reflex. His eyes were shadowed in the dimness, his teeth gleamed.

"Relax. I'm going to boost you up." And he did it, as easily as he'd hefted the flashlight. She found herself sitting on the edge of the stage, looking down at him, her eyes an inch or two above the top of his head.

"Thanks." Her voice sounded unnaturally loud in the dimness.

But he didn't move away.

Thea's pulse quickened. Brady reached out to rest his hands above her knees, where her short skirt ended. Slowly, deliberately, he shifted closer, stepping between her parted thighs. Shadows cloaked his face, leaving only his voice.

"When are we going to work this out, Thea?"

The words were soft, very nearly a whisper. To hear them at all, she found herself pressing her forehead to his, so that for a moment they stood touching. And her breath shuddered out.

It was inevitable, that was all there was to it. She couldn't think why it was that she'd wanted to keep him at bay. The rest of the world, the rest of her life didn't seem real. The only thing that mattered was here, this moment, this cone of light, enclosing the two of them. What she wanted was him, what she wanted was this.

And she was taking it.

Thea laid her hands over Brady's, slid them up his arms, over his shoulders to meet behind his neck. Her answer wasn't in words but in the language of heat, desire, surrender.

Triumph.

HE'D KNOWN HUNGER, Brady thought feverishly. He'd wanted throughout the endless days, woken up in the night, dry-mouthed with need for her. He'd lived with the ache like sharp rocks in his belly.

None of it was even close to what he felt now.

Her mouth, that wide, full, impossibly soft mouth was open against his, demanding even as she gave, luring him in with taste and touch. She nipped at his lips, skimmed her own along his jaw, down his throat even as her fingers reached for the buttons of his shirt.

He'd thought she'd been open that first night together but it had been nothing compared to this. Perhaps it was that his memory paled in comparison to the fire and flash of the now. Perhaps it was that having finally made the decision to be with him, knowing him, she was throwing herself into it utterly in a way that hadn't been possible before.

The noise she made deep in her throat held equal parts exhilaration and abandon, and threatened his control. The way she wrapped her legs around his waist as though to pull him closer nearly overmastered him. And then she pushed his shirt off his shoulders and he knew he had to move or go past the point of no return.

"Slide closer," Brady murmured. The words echoed in the silence of the theater and Thea raised her head.

"What?"

"Slide closer." His hands slipped around her hips to pull her toward him and she went. Then again, in that instant, she'd have responded the same way to anything he asked of her.

The heat of his bare torso against her legs made her take a breath. As though the dimness made him want to learn her by touch, he ran his hands up her body, over her hips, along her waist, feeling her through the fabric. Then his fingers worked up beneath her skirt and he began pulling down the satiny wisp of fabric beneath.

"What are you—"

"Shhh. Working space," he said and bent closer to her. And with a sort of incredulous delight, she felt him drape her legs over his shoulders. "Playing doctor," he murmured. "Just lie back and tell me where it hurts."

"It's a little stiff there doctor," she said, sliding her fingers down to the tops of her thighs.

He gave a short laugh. "Trust me, it's stiff in lots of places. Let me get in there and take a closer look, shall we?"

"But doctor, it's dark."

"Then I'll go by feel." He curved his hands over the tops of her thighs.

In the dimness, lying back, Thea couldn't see, she could only wait to feel. Anticipation made her nerve endings hyperacute. His cheeks brushed against her inner thighs and she sucked in a breath. When his breath heated those tender lips below the curls of hair, she shivered.

Then the tip of his tongue touched her and she jolted and cried out.

"Clearly you're in some distress," he said. "I'd better examine you further."

With his tongue, he traced a furrow between her inner lips. In all the years she'd been pleasuring herself, she'd never realized how sensitive that fragile flesh could be, but she discovered it now as he drew first one side then the other into his mouth, tonguing the delicate skin, moving his head to draw his lips over them. She moaned helplessly.

But he wasn't finished. He licked again, going deeper, working closer and closer to what he sought, to the pearl in the oyster, the engorged bead of her clitoris. And when he found it, the bolt of sensation shot through her with the suddenness of an electrical shock. This time the moan was a strangled cry, the sound amplified in the empty auditorium. And then he pressed his mouth against her fully, hot and questing.

And relentless.

Thea twisted, her hands flying down to clutch his shoulders. His tongue was doing devilish things, delicious things, wonderful things, fluttering against her clit. He traced swirling patterns, bringing her closer and closer to some nameless destination, filling her with that invisible, magical, glorious pleasure until she didn't think she could bear any more. Yet she managed more, and more, and more before she exploded with it, crying out and shuddering against him.

"I want to be in you now," Brady said raggedly.

"The stage?"

"Too high."

"Standing?"

He glanced around and got a wicked look on his face. "I've got a better idea." He drew her down from the stage, walked her across to an upright chair that had been discarded along with some other furniture. "Props," he said.

"Over the top," Thea said.

"Not nearly enough. Just wait."

He kissed her without hands. Then she heard the sound of foil ripping and she understood that he'd been going for his wallet. His shirt was long gone. His belt was cool against her fingers, his zipper cooler. She could feel how hard he was. When she would have drawn him out, he stilled her hands. When she would have dropped to her knees, he caught at her arms. "Later," he said, and easing his jeans down, sat.

Thea stepped forward and leaned over him to fuse her mouth to his, hands gripping the knobs at the top of the chair. For a moment, the kiss was her universe, the heat, the drive, the want. And then she wanted more, needed him in her with an ache that went bone deep. Stepping forward, she straddled him. She felt the brush of the tip of his cock, impossibly soft, impossibly hard as he rubbed it through the slick cleft between her legs, getting himself wet, finding the opening that led to the core of her.

And then she sank down on him and he shoved himself up into her to the hilt.

It tore a moan from her throat, a moan that merged with his muffled groan. Thea wrapped her arms around his neck and pressed herself against him. He filled her. Every fiber of them was brought together in a way that was entirely pleasurable and entirely new. For a moment, it was enough. And then she began to move.

Shock, jubilance and absolute, utter ecstasy.

Never before. She'd never felt it like this, never, never, never. Orgasm had always been something that came from the hand, the mouth. Intercourse, as much as she loved it, was about a different mix of sensations. It couldn't push her up that slope of rising tension until she came.

But now, oh, now something in the way they were positioned pressed her clit right against the shaft of his cock. With every rise and fall, Thea felt the stroke of him against that sensitive bud of nerves, like he was touching her or licking her only better. Longer. Slicker. Hotter.

Harder.

Every stroke dragged her closer and closer to orgasm. With every stroke, her arousal deepened. She felt him inside, she felt him outside, around her, in her, on her. She was crying out, half sobbing her pleasure and she couldn't help it. Feeling him hard and thick inside her, feeling that stroke, that rub, that touch, it was going to send her over, even as he was inside her, so deep inside, filling her until there was nothing more to be felt. His mouth was on her breast, sucking the nipple, nipping it with his teeth as she moved up and down feverishly, trying to hold on to every instant of that incredible sensation. Then as though she were physically flung, she went over without warning, shuddering and clutching at him as she contracted around him, as the hot pleasure washed through her, exploded out to her fingertips.

BRADY FELT HER contracting around his cock, heard her cries and knew what had happened, *knew it.* The proof of her pleasure, the powerful pressure around him, the slick slide and helpless shaking dragged him over the edge. He pulled her down on himself hard, spilling himself in her as she still shuddered with her own release.

He couldn't move, Brady thought. Every muscle had been drained in the orgasm and Thea lay draped against him.

"Where's a bed when you need one," she asked.

"Forget about beds," Brady said. "I want this chair. I'm thinking of having it bronzed. And a little plaque added to the back—'Never Say Never.'"

"Truer words," Thea said. "Truer words." She shifted slightly. "Now, about who gets to keep this chair…"

10

MORNING LIGHT SHONE red through her closed eyelids. Consciousness was not far behind. And after consciousness, memory.

Hell.

Or déjà vu. Except when Thea opened her eyes this time, she saw not an unknown male space, but the familiar soft green walls of Robyn's guest room. The usual botanical prints hung by the window, the blue and white pressed-tin sign still advertised Little Fairy soap.

And behind her, with his arms wrapped around her, lay Brady.

Thea sighed. Bringing him back to the house the night before had seemed like a good idea. That was the problem with morning, she thought, glaring at the light that filtered through the half-open blinds.

Holding her breath, she eased away from him experimentally. Brady inhaled and rolled onto his back, throwing one arm over his eyes. In a moment, his breathing became deep and regular. Asleep, she decided in relief and shifted again.

His hand whipped out and caught her wrist. He said something—at least she thought they were words, but they were pretty much unintelligible.

"What?"

"Are you one of those morning people?"

"I wake up early."

"You're sick."

"Then you won't want me around," she replied, tugging her wrist away.

Only to find it held fast. "You're not by any chance thinking of trying your disappearing act again, are you?" One green eye opened to study her. "Because I'll sic Darlene on you if I have to."

"Oh hell, Darlene," she said, sitting upright.

"You don't get to bolt twice."

She shook her head. "You don't understand. If Darlene doesn't get out, I'm going to be hunting down a rug-cleaning service."

"Just put her in the backyard," he suggested, moving onto his side to watch her as she hastily dragged on shorts and a T-shirt.

"Nope. The family on the other side of the duplex owns the place—and the backyard. Ixnay on Darlene, and specifically on Darlene byproducts. Besides, I'd still have to go out with a shovel or something. It's easier to just deal with it." She hopped on one foot as she slipped on a tennis shoe. "Go back to sleep. This is my problem."

Brady looked at her resignedly and flipped back the sheet. "No way. As sure as I let you out of my sight, you'll get busy manufacturing fifty thousand reasons why we can't have sex again, and since I personally am planning to get you naked as soon and as often as I can, I can't afford to let that happen."

He plucked his shirt off the floor and eyed her suspiciously. "So if I turn my back, are you going to vanish?"

Thea rolled her eyes. "I won't vanish."

"Swear?"

She stepped quickly over to him and drew him into a long, lingering kiss. "There. Satisfied?"

He looked down at his cock, already thickening. "Not even close. What would you say to—"

There was a low whine outside the door. "Looking after Darlene so she doesn't burst, and waiting for you to catch up?" Thea hurried to the door. "Absolutely." She blew him a kiss and stepped into the hall.

IT WAS A BEAUTIFUL MORNING, not too chilly, not too hot. Thea sat down on the warm, worn wood of the front steps, enjoying the early sun.

"This wasn't very smart, you know," she told Darlene as she watched her sniff and mark her favorite bushes. "You're supposed to be my friend and talk me out of dumb stuff."

Darlene seemed to be far more interested in the rhododendron.

"But that chair trick, boy, that was something amazing."

Oh, yeah, that chair trick was a life-changer. Actually, all things considered, the situation really wasn't that bad. No, she hadn't planned to sleep with him again. No, it wasn't the measured, sane relationship she'd been hoping for. Then again, she hardly trusted herself to be a good judge of that anyway.

And she'd had a hell of a good time.

What did it really matter, Thea thought, watching the little dog. It wasn't like she was staying in Portland, no matter how cool it was. A month, month and a half and she'd be back home. In the meantime, she had a place of

her own, or at least Robyn's place, and it wasn't as if her
job depended on Brady. It was okay. It was safe.

She could walk away whenever she needed to.

Maybe he was right. Maybe she had been overcomplicating things. Maybe it was as easy as just having a good
time and trusting that they could keep things separate. Fun
while it lasted, Brady seemed to specialize in that. And
when she went home, no harm, no foul.

Of course, that was the classic setup, sex without strings.
And the plot of a thousand romances when the strings spon-
taneously formed anyway. In this particular case though, she
was leaving, and it would take a lot of string to reach from
Portland to L.A.

Anyway, a guy like Brady wasn't built for serious. She
suspected Brady had done sex without strings any number
of times, happily. For her, it would be a chance to get back
in practice, have some fun on a limited scale. A dry run for
the real business of finding her future.

In the meantime, there was the chair thing.

She heard the door behind her open and Brady came out.
"Morning, Sunshine," she said with a grin.

He growled at her and went to his Jeep to dig out a baseball
hat and sunglasses. "Do you really do this every morning?"

"Every morning, plastic baggies and all." She clipped
on Darlene's leash. "Come on, it's an outdoors thing. You
should like it."

"I would, if it were happening like two hours later."

"Oh, come on, six isn't that early."

He glowered at her. "It's five forty-five."

"Darlene waits for no man." Thea led the dog out the
gate to meet him on the sidewalk. "Don't sulk. We'll be
back in half an hour and you can go home and sleep."

"Go home? You're kicking me out?" In a flash, he'd pulled her to him. "I told you," he murmured against her mouth as her knees turned to water, "I've got plans for you. And I noticed, Robyn's got herself some nice kitchen chairs."

Kitchen chairs. "In that case, let's get this walk over with," Thea managed weakly.

HE DIDN'T REALLY MIND getting up early all that much, Brady had to admit. He'd been doing it all week anyway. And he was a pragmatic enough man to look on the good side when he didn't have a choice—he was outdoors, he was with a beautiful woman and there was the promise of sex later. Hell, it didn't get much better than that.

For a while, it was just enough to walk and wake up, enjoying the sun and the presence of Thea at his side. Darlene's claws ticked on the pavement. A bird whistled somewhere nearby. He caught a glimpse of Mount Hood rising in the distance and gauged his chances of getting Thea out for a hike.

"So doesn't walking Darlene give you the urge to get another dog?" Thea asked, catching his glance.

"Walking Darlene makes me glad I have a backyard and a doggie door."

"Surely even then you'd take the dog out."

"Heck yeah. I used to take Spike mountain biking with me all the time. He had a great time cruising around, chasing squirrels."

"He was your buddy," she said softly.

"He was. I'll probably look for another one just like him. Border collies are smart, tough. I like that. I've got a friend that breeds them."

"Purebred?"

"Yeah, sure. Why?" He tucked his hands in his back pockets.

"They have lots of smart, tough dogs at the animal shelter," she pointed out.

"Adopt a pet?" He glanced at her, amused.

"Why not? It fits with Portland—reuse, renew, recycle."

"We'll, maybe I'll—" Brady stopped dead, staring. "What the hell is that?"

The yard in question was a sea of green—gravel, that was. Grass, bushes, trees, all gone. A pair of neatly tended petunia beds up by the front porch softened the house. And in the center of the artfully raked gravel, on a shrinelike pedestal, stood a lawnmower—spray-painted gold.

Thea cleared her throat. "I believe that's a statement of personal freedom."

"I guess." Brady grinned as they crossed the street. "You gotta love this town. Too bad you weren't here about ten years ago. They had the twenty-four-hour Church of Elvis downtown."

"The Church of Elvis?"

"Not a real church. A storefront in a downtown gallery. Coin operated," he added. "You could read messages on the sacred Elvis monitor, see the miracle of the spinning Elvises. Even try to call him."

"In heaven?"

"At Graceland."

"And here I thought it was the weather that Portland had going for it."

He gave her a look over the top of his sunglasses. "No need to take potshots."

"I was serious," she protested.

"Careful, now. It's easy to say that in summertime. It's the winter that really shows you what Portland is. Try six straight months of Portland mist and then tell me you like it."

"You don't?"

He gave a careless shrug. "It's weather. That's what happens when you've got sky. I figure outdoors is good no matter what's coming down. Then again, I grew up here. Imports tend to have problems adjusting."

"Imports, huh?"

"Yeah."

"I think I'd like it," Thea said, watching Darlene sniff at the base of a maple.

And he wondered why that interested him so much. "Big talk."

"Trust me, I grew up in the desert. Water falling from the sky is good."

It was the first time she'd ever told him anything about herself voluntarily. "Desert, huh? Whereabouts?"

"Blythe. In the southeast corner of California, down by Arizona and the border," she went on at his look of incomprehension.

"What's it like?"

"About what you'd expect. Barren, dry. And hot? You have no idea. The temperature breaks a hundred pretty much every day in the summer."

Brady whistled. "Not sure I'd go for a steady diet of that. Although I'd approve of you in a bikini. Or out of it," he added as she swatted at him.

"The desert's beautiful, don't get me wrong, but I love rain. I really, really love rain."

"Why live in L.A. then?"

"My people are there," she said simply.

"Your family?" She'd cracked the door; he figured he'd nudge it open a little more.

She gave a short, humorless laugh. "No. My friends. My sister lives in the Bay Area."

"What about your parents?"

She moved a shoulder. "Just a phone call away."

And somehow he had the feeling she didn't make that phone call very often.

"So, what, you grew up in Blythe and then moved to L.A., right? College?" he guessed.

She nodded. "That's where I met my friends. Doing a school play."

"What, you were an actor?"

"No, I was into dance. Modern, jazz. I was going to live my life on the stage."

"And that's where you met Robyn."

"Well, I—"

Just then, a frenzy of enraged barking and snarling and black-and-tan motion exploded behind the fence of a house up ahead. Darlene lunged against her collar, adding her own high-pitched yelps to the mix, fighting to get her face right up to the slats and what resolved itself as a big, tough, muscled rottweiler.

"You've gotta give Darlene her props, she's not backing down," Brady said, admiring Thea's arms as she dragged the dog back.

"Girl don't take trash talking from no one. 'You want a piece of *me,* prison boy?'" Thea grinned. "It's funny, though, she knows this dog. It's gotta be something about the fence. When he's outside or they're in the park, they're the best of buddies. I guess he's territorial."

Brady pulled her to his side as they walked on. "We guys

are like that." He let his arm down to capture her hand. "So you studied dance?"

Thea wrapped Darlene's leash around her hand a few times. "What's this, let's hear Thea's life story?"

"I'm curious."

She shook her head. "Trust me, it's not that interesting. You now, that's different. I bet the history of the McMillan clan's got more than a few good stories in it."

Patience, Brady reminded himself. It was all a matter of time. "You want McMillan stories?"

She nodded.

"Well, there was the time Michael and I went down to the McCall Park fountain with a bottle of dishwashing liquid. We were going to make bubbles," he explained.

"Oh, this one, I've got to hear," she said as they turned toward home.

"NOW, THIS IS THE PALETTE for the rooms and upper floors." Dana Stadler, the interior designer, laid the sheet of paint chips and swatches before Brady.

They sat at a table that had been thrown up on the raised platform that was destined to be the theater's restaurant. Somewhere, a radio was blasting classic rock over the sounds of hammers and drills.

"Have you had a chance to think some more about the stage-set concept I laid out last week?" Dana asked. She reminded him of k.d. lang, only her suits were twice as sharp. She pointed to the sketch with one short, unpainted fingernail. "I really think it would work. We could play with partial backdrops or props to give drama to the rooms."

"I was thinking of something else," he said.

"Really?" Her voice was scrupulously professional but a tad cool. "Like what?"

"Well, playing off tango, first of all. Costumes, music, art. But down here, maybe working the dressing room angle."

"The dressing room angle?"

"Yeah. Either use the real rooms or add new ones on the far side of the stage, where the storage rooms are now." The more he'd thought about the idea, the more he'd liked it.

Dana flipped through some papers. "That wasn't in the original plan."

"Nope, but someone in our group came up with the idea and I'm going to run with it."

"You're going to run with what?" a voice said from behind him. Michael's voice.

Brady waited a beat, then turned. "A-ha, look who's here. Happened to be in the neighborhood?"

"No, I figured I'd sit in." Michael pulled up an extra chair.

Kitchen chair, Brady thought, and worked to force his mind elsewhere. "Showing up at the contractor launch meeting, inspecting in the mornings, sitting in on design. Boy, you know, for a guy who didn't have the bandwidth for this project, you're sure in the middle of it."

"I'm not in the middle of it," Michael countered. "I'm merely keeping an eye on things."

"An eye on things," Brady repeated. "Including me."

"Not you, the project. So this new room idea, maybe you and I should talk about it before we move forward with Dana, here. Dana," Michael continued, "you all right with taking ten?"

She glanced up from the notes she'd been conspicuously concentrating on. "Fine with me. Is there a place around here I can get coffee?"

"Left out the front door and take the next left," Michael responded before Brady could open his mouth. "Good scones."

"I'll bring you back a couple."

Brady studied Michael as she walked away. "Been around here a lot, I guess."

"Off and on. So what's this about new rooms?"

It wasn't worth being frustrated. Michael was being Michael; it was his money at stake, too. "It goes with the theme. The backstage idea works all right, but it's not enough."

"What do you mean?"

"At the Lincoln School, we turned classrooms into guest rooms. We could do the same thing here by playing on the dressing room angle. I'm not talking about a huge number, just three or four. Call 'em the premium suites. We can turn the storage rooms over on the other side into real dressing rooms for the performers—no way are we going to need to store costumes and props and stuff."

"What are we looking at for cost?"

He had that, had crunched through numbers all morning after feverish consults with the architect and contractor. "Five percent over our current budget. Pay for itself in two years of occupancy."

Michael mulled it over. Finally, he nodded. "Okay, let's do it. Good idea," he added.

"It wasn't mine. Thea came up with it."

"Thea?"

"The tango dancer."

"Ah. You bringing on consultants, now?"

"You know I am. Tango's an integral part of the theme."

"And is she the babe from the park?"

Brady gave Michael a sharp look. "She's the dancer, yeah. The tango studio that ran the dance is on board to provide an entertainment program for us. Thea works there."

"She's got a lot of opinions about the theater for never having seen it."

"I brought her over a couple of nights ago to answer a couple of questions about the stage."

"A couple of nights ago?" Michael repeated.

"She has a job. That's when we could get here."

"I heard you brought a date into the Cascade Brewery. That her?"

Brady's brows rose. "Chatty bunch we've got over there."

"You're an owner. People notice what the owners do."

"And report it, apparently."

"That shouldn't come as a surprise." Michael nodded his head to the beat of a Pearl Jam song playing behind them. "Brady, we've got a lot of money riding on this project," he said abruptly. "Make sure you're paying attention to what's important. And the difference between business and pleasure. We can't afford to screw this up."

Brady's jaw tightened. He looked at the stage, then back at Michael. "Don't worry about the project. It'll get done."

"Just make sure that's all that gets done."

Brady gave him a level stare. "I'd say that's between her and me."

"Oh, man." Michael sighed.

Just then, Dana walked up with a bag and a carrier tray holding three coffees. "Okay, I'm back with ammo. We going to talk design, guys?"

Muscle by muscle, Brady forced himself to relax. "Yeah we're going to talk design."

11

THEA SAT ON THE SWING on Robyn's front porch, one foot tucked under her, the other dangling down as she swayed gently. On a pad in her lap, she scribbled notes for a tango showcase. If teaching was her first love, choreography was her second, turning imagination into movement, shepherding the flow of the dance.

Rough out an opening night program for the theater, Brady had requested, so she'd designed showcases, enlisted the efforts of the tango society in supplying performers. Now it was a matter of putting the finishing touches on at her end. And soon, she'd be one of the performers on stage.

Darlene lay in the shade at her feet, panting in an adenoidal manner. Not that the day was all that hot; it was still morning. Then again, pugs didn't have all that much of a nose and snout to cool down with. Thermally challenged, Thea thought, reaching down to rub the dog's ears. Darlene was also metabolically challenged, which meant that a walk in the afternoon, when things cooled down again, would be good. They could haul Brady along, in case of exhaustion.

A smile curved her mouth. They'd gone hiking in Forest Park days before. Or at least Brady and Thea had; Darlene had started flagging after maybe a quarter of a mile. Brady had wound up carrying the tired thing the rest of the way, refusing to answer to anything but Brady Sherpa.

A night's sleep—and she let him sleep a fair bit, she didn't know what he was complaining about—had seemed to revive him. Surely he'd have recovered by now. She was pretty confident she'd be able to lure him along again.

At her side, her cell phone burbled. "Hello?" she answered.

"Hey, tango lady."

Somehow the day was brighter when she was talking with him. "Hey, yourself," she said, grinning like an idiot. "You worked late last night, huh?"

"The beer waits for no man. Hope you didn't stay up. I was hoping to make it by but brewing took a lot longer than I expected."

"No, I crashed," she said lightly. And if she'd lain awake in the darkness listening for a knock, that was her problem.

"How's our champion hiker?" he asked.

She reached down to Darlene, who'd jumped to her feet and was wiggling happily at the sound of Brady's voice over the phone. "I think she's recovered and ready for further punishment."

"How about you? You up for a bike ride?"

"A bike ride?"

"Sure. It'll be fun. Fresh air, exercise, change of scenery. And I'll feed you lunch," he played his trump card.

"Lunch?" It was tempting, but… "Robyn's bike has a broken chain."

"You can use one of mine. I've got an extra. The trail's about fifteen miles, cutting up through the Columbia River Gorge. You'll like it."

She glanced down at her pad. "I'm in the middle of working on your opening night stuff," she protested.

"We can talk about it as we ride. Anyway, there's time. A couple of hours won't make or break."

"It better not be too many hours. My classes start at four. And anyway, you've got to be at work, don't you?"

"The beer's fine and I'm leaving the theater right now. I've got some comp time coming. Come on," he wheedled, "play hooky with me. It'll be fun."

"Okay," she said, abandoning her protests.

"Great. See you in five." And with a click, he disconnected.

That was Brady. He had a disconcerting tendency to pop up and try to persuade her to set any plans aside—and an even more disconcerting tendency to get her to agree. Maybe it was the laughter that was always lurking in his voice. Maybe it was the way fun followed him.

And she knew she was going to miss him when she was gone.

The phone rang again. "What do you want now?"

"You have a helmet?" Brady asked.

"I'll use Robyn's."

"I bet you'll look cute in it. See you."

"Not if I see you first," she said.

"Feisty, huh? I like 'em like that," he said and disconnected.

The phone rang again and she snatched it up without looking. "Jeez, stop calling me," she said with a grin.

"What the hell kind of way is that to answer the phone?" The words hit her with the force of a slap; then again, conversations with her father usually did.

"I'm sorry." Her voice went flat. "I thought you were someone else." Rude shock. It was like having a bucket of ice emptied over her.

"Just because you're all grown up, doesn't mean you can say whatever you want to people. Particularly your parents."

She massaged the bridge of her nose. "Again, I'm sorry. What can I do for you?"

"Get rid of that smart mouth, for starters."

"Hello, Father. How are you?"

"Good enough. Your mother's not doing so well, though. You'd know that if you ever bothered to call."

Betty Mitchell hadn't "been herself" for the past fifteen years. Given the way Thea's father had treated her—not significantly differently than he'd treated them all—it wasn't a surprise. Not that he'd ever admit it. Hoyt Mitchell was never at fault for anything.

"You know her, alway whining," her father continued, now that he was rolling. "She's found a doctor who wants her to have heart surgery at the end of the month."

"Heart surgery?" She blinked.

"A bypass. She doesn't seem any more wheezy than usual, but they want her in pronto. So you and your sister had better get down here for it."

The end of the month, Thea thought, trying to remember the date of Robyn's return. "I'll try. I'm on a special job up in Portland right now. I don't know if I can get away."

Her father's voice rose. "I don't give a damn what you're doing. You've never had a job worth spit in your life. Now, this is your mother. You find a way to get here to take care of her, do you hear me?"

Translation: so Hoyt wouldn't have to. But it was heart surgery, Thea thought.

"I'll figure something out," she said. "Is there a hotel near the hospital?"

"You'll be right here in case your mother needs you. Your old bed will do fine," he snapped impatiently.

And, nauseated with herself, she found herself caving. It wasn't worth the fight.

Thea let out a breath. "Is Mom around so I can say hi?"

"She's asleep. You can call her later, if your dialing fingers aren't broken. Now here are the dates of the surgery."

Obediently, Thea wrote them down.

"I want you here two days before that," her father concluded. At that, there was nothing further to say and mercifully, he disconnected.

She was shaking, she thought, staring at her hands dispassionately. That was always the way of it. Hoyt Mitchell, autocrat, clinging to bitterness and hostility as though it were a holy calling. It was one thing when she called them—she was prepared for it. To get smacked by it out of the blue, though, that was worse.

She'd grown up with his constant verbal abuse. It didn't matter that a dozen years had passed since she'd lived under the same roof as him, more than a dozen years since she'd been under his control. She was no better than Pavlov's dog—when she heard his voice, eighteen years of conditioning kicked in and she found herself knuckling under.

I'll be seventy-five and he'll be eighty and he'll still be acting like my big brother.

Some habits you couldn't outgrow.

She'd always figured she would, though. That she'd leave and never go back, that she'd never wind up around someone like him. And she'd gotten involved with men who stirred her. But like a slow motion horror movie scene, there was always that moment in any relationship when the guy she thought was so wonderful suddenly morphed into Hoyt and she realized that she'd walked right into it again. Boyfriends in high school. Boyfriends in college.

Derek.

Thea glanced out at the street, waiting for her stomach to stop roiling. It was a neighborhood for families. Pretty yards, neat houses. How many of them were really window dressing to cover up fathers who twisted their children's minds and hearts and emotions? Not all abuse involved fists and bodies. Sometimes words were destructive enough.

When she saw Brady drive up, her first thought was that she wasn't ready. She needed space. She needed time to let the effects of the conversation bleed away. She needed to not be around any guy just then. But he got out, grinning in his ballcap and sunglasses. Darlene was up and barking happily before he even reached the gate. Thea rose.

"Hey, where are your clothes?"

"On my body," she said as they met on the porch.

"That can be rectified if we go inside," he pointed out and reached for her. When she shifted slightly, he took a better look and frowned. "You okay? Did something happen?"

Thea shook her head. "No, nothing. I'm fine. Call from home, that's all."

"Everything okay?"

Was it ever? "Yeah, sure, fine. I'm thinking I might skip the ride, though."

He studied her a moment. "I think you should go. Do you good to get out and get your mind off whatever. All those endorphins, and lunch. Not to mention my undeniably charming self." He slipped his arms around her. And somehow against the heat of his body, she found herself agreeing.

Once they got on the road, she was glad she had. Life was too short to spend the time brooding, and brooding was what she would have done. No point, she decided. It wasn't like it would change anything; she was better off focusing on the good stuff.

So instead, she pedaled down the road. At first, she was too busy getting used to the shifters and the brakes on Brady's nifty eighteen-speed road bike to notice much of anything. As they left the city, though, traffic and noise fell away and they rode side by side, taking their time. Her father's influence ebbed with the traffic. Finally, she could breathe. And she mentally blessed Brady for understanding intuitively what she needed.

"You know in L.A. it takes at least an hour to get out of the city any way you go, unless you're diving into the ocean," Thea said idly.

"Hard to bike under water."

"You said it."

"Never been to L.A.," he added.

"I don't know that it's your kind of place. There's nothing you can get there that you can't here, except maybe sun. Portland's amazing. So much to offer and yet it's still small, at least compared to what I'm used to."

"Part of what I like about it."

The road wound through a forest of mostly evergreens. The wood stretched out around them, tree after tree, tall, short, broad, narrow, in a thousand shades of brown and green. Beneath, the fallen needles formed a rust-colored carpet that looked soft and yielding.

"What are all these, pines?" Thea asked.

"The ones with the black trunks are Doug fir," Brady said as they rode.

"Lot of them."

"They're good at competing. Where they do well, they do really well. Otherwise, you've got some maple, alder. That one with the reddish trunk over there is a Ponderosa." He flashed a smile. "My favorite tree."

He would have a favorite tree, she thought. Brady might seem slapdash but she'd begun to realize that he took nothing in his world for granted.

And when she saw the redwood sign, she understood. It was big, with a nineteen fifties flavor. At the bottom, a stylized sketch showed a sprawling lodge. Over the top arced the words Brimfield Farm.

"Brimfield," she exclaimed. "This is you guys."

"Last time I checked."

As they wound down the secondary road, the forest fell away to expose a broad valley bracketed by hills. Ahead, she saw the parallel rows of a grape vinyard marching up the hillside overlooking the patchwork green of a truck farm, complete with tall, latticed windmill. In the midst of it all stood a collection of Craftsman-style buildings that had her thinking of CCC structures built during the Great Depression. It felt like a refuge, it felt hours away from the city. Above all, it held a sense of peace.

She could feel more of the tension easing away.

"Oh, Brady, this is wonderful."

"I thought you might like it. Let me show you around."

They got off their bikes and walked them up to a rack before the main structure. The building wasn't ornate like the theater, or imposing like the Lincoln School. It was just unpretentious, open and comfortable.

They'd carried through the Depression-era theme in the wide halls with WPA style murals, the themes simple, the colors vivid. In contrast, the rooms provided soothing havens in tones of oatmeal, stone gray, raffia. She felt as if she should check in and stay for a few days, then she'd be back to her old self.

"This seems like a great weekend getaway," Thea said as they walked back out into the hall.

Brady came up behind her and wrapped his arms around her waist. "If we didn't have to go back to work, we could stay."

"Mmm. But we do."

"Slave driver," he accused and moved away.

And Thea's mouth dropped open. "Did you just grope me?" she demanded, her breast still tingling from his squeeze.

"Who, me?" Brady blinked at her guilelessly.

"Yes, you."

"I'm sure you must be mistaken."

Her lips twitched. "I don't think so. I distinctly felt a grope."

"It wasn't me."

"Then who was it?"

He checked the empty hallway, thought for a moment. "The ghost," he said quickly.

"The ghost?" She did her best to raise an eyebrow.

"Yeah, we have a ghost here, a worker who, uh, died in a tragic fruit-picking accident and ever since he flits around the place."

"Groping the guests."

"Checking for ripeness."

"A tragic fruit-picking accident?"

"Why don't we go outside and see the grounds?" he said hastily.

"Get away from the groping ghost."

"Maybe," he said, giving her ass a surreptitious squeeze as she stepped out the door.

"Was that—?"

"What?"

"Never mind," she muttered.

It had turned into one of those idyllic summer days, Thea thought, warm, lazy and quiet. If she held still, she swore she could hear things growing. In the farm, zucchini and summer squash ran wild. The pepper and tomato plants looked as if they were hung with red, yellow and orange jewels. Behind the garden wound the rows of the grapes, and past it, a field of pale green.

Thea pointed. "What's that?"

"Canola. We run biodiesel out here. It's not much good without the bio part."

"Why not use regular power?"

"This way, we make our own." He shrugged. "I kind of like the whole idea of sustainability. It took a while to talk Michael into it, but it pays off eventually. We grow our own vegetables and fruit. We get our beef from a rancher who uses the mash left over from our brewing as cattle feed. It all kind of comes full circle."

"It's beautiful." She looked around to see the Cascades, snow still on the shoulders of some of the peaks. "So which mountains am I looking at?"

He squinted, then got behind her and pointed over her shoulder so she could sight along his arm. "That's Mount St. Helens."

"As in the one that erupted?"

"As in. And that one over there is Mount Adams. I tried climbing it once."

"I didn't know you were into climbing."

"A buddy took me up in the winter. Trust me, freezing my butt off for a week was enough to cure me of it. Give me rock climbing, any day."

That was where he'd developed his strong, tough hands, she realized.

Trees, mountains, roads and plants. She gave him a sidelong glance. "Is there anything you don't know about this area?"

"What do you mean?"

"It's like it's your backyard, you know it so well. I like it."

Brady looked flummoxed. "Why wouldn't I? This is where I grew up. It's where I live."

"A lot of people don't care. In L.A.? You'd be lucky if they could identify a eucalyptus, even if it is in their own backyard."

"In L.A., there's not that much to identify. Maybe you should give up and move here," Brady said, keeping his voice casual.

"How about the stuff on the trellises out there?" Thea asked as though she hadn't heard him.

"Hops. For the beer."

He'd planted them on slanting frames that rose a good three feet higher than his head, each vine twining vigorously up the cables. They were going to be ready soon, Brady saw in satisfaction, leaning in to finger the papery yellow cone of the fruit and crush it between his fingers.

"Watch out. The owners will get you for that."

"I've got official dispensation."

"Official?" She gave him a skeptical look.

"All right, I'll 'fess up. I said I was playing hooky but I really wanted to come out and check to see if we're getting close to harvest."

She watched him inspect another plant. "You could buy them like other people do. Save yourself some trouble."

"Who wants to be like other people? Besides, this way, I get the kind I want. Plus, I know that no one's chemical crud is going to get into my beer."

"A purist."

"About the stuff that counts," he agreed.

BRADY REACHED OUT and caught her hand. The bees and cicadas set up a somnolent buzz in the background. As he walked with her down between the rows, the heady scent rose around them.

"I'm glad you came out with me. I wanted you to see it," he said. And he'd wanted to be the one to show it to her. Sure, he could say the snap decision to go for a ride was because he'd been stir crazy, but he hadn't just wanted to get out, he'd wanted to get out with Thea.

That had been before he'd gotten to her house and seen the shadows in her eyes, the somberness that hovered around the corners of her mouth.

"It's so beautiful around here, the way everything's green and growing. Where I came from, the only way anything grows is with irrigation."

"Blythe? What do they grow around there?"

"Cotton, winter vegetables."

"Did your family farm?"

She gave a short laugh. "Uh, no. My dad's not the farmer type." And that quickly, the shadows were back.

"What does he do?" he asked as they neared the end of the row. His voice was casual; his eyes, as he watched her, were not.

"He's a mechanic." She made a noise that wasn't quite

a laugh. "He's good at making things do what he wants them to."

To ask or not?

"He was the one you were talking with, wasn't he?"

She hesitated. "Yes."

"Something wrong at home?"

Thea took a few more steps in silence, then tugged her hand loose and walked out to the open space beyond the end of the row. The grapevines curved across the hillsides. The canola flowed with the breeze like water. She stood there, staring out over the valley.

"Look at it," she said as though she hadn't heard him. "I don't think you could ever be unhappy living with a view like this." She turned to face him, eyes unnaturally bright. "So, I seem to remember someone promising me lunch."

He started to protest. Something told him to let it go.

For now.

"We could go get some lunch."

"Good." She stepped in close to him, close enough to skim her lips over his. As though released by the summer sun, her scent whispered around him. And her secrets. "So you're one of the owners here, right?"

"Yep."

"Do you think we might be able to go back and tour another room? I feel a real need to do some two person meditation."

"I think we could look into that," he said, a smile breaking over his face.

And felt a very firm squeeze on his cock. He blinked in surprise.

"Did you just grope me?"

"Must have been that ghost," she said primly.

12

"It's GETTING DANGEROUS to hang around you people," Delaney said.

Seven women sprawled around the living room of Cilla's Brentwood home. Once, they'd lived there as college housemates. Now, they were back to celebrate with Kelly the night before her wedding to Kev Cooper.

"What did we do?" Trish asked as she came back from the table Cilla had set up as a mini bar with fresh orange juice and champagne on ice.

"Betrayed me," Delaney explained. "We used to be hot chicks on the loose. Now, what, Cilla and Sabrina are married, Kelly's got one foot down the aisle—and a bun in the oven, I might add. You're living with Ty." Here, she glowered at Trish. "Paige isn't living with Zach but she might as well be. Hell, Thea, you and I are the only ones left. It's a sad day." Delaney shook her head and upended her glass to get the last swallow before rising to get more.

"I love mimosas," Kelly said wistfully.

"That's why we're drinking them for you, sweetie," Sabrina said, leaning over to give her a kiss. "It's your bachelorette party. After this, we'll dial up some porn on cable—"

"Oooh, goodie, the Home Shopping Network," Cilla squealed.

"Uh, Cilla, honey, we're talking about the real thing," Delaney said. "You know, naked guys, cocks, blow jobs?"

"You choose your porn and I'll choose mine," Cilla retorted haughtily.

"Anyway we're celebrating for you tonight and then you get a rain check," Sabrina continued. "And after you give birth to little Elmo—"

"I thought we picked Chester," Delaney called.

"No, it was Maynard," Trish corrected, then frowned and blinked owlishly at her glass. "I'm almost sure it was Maynard."

"You're all evil," Kelly told them, "trying to give my sweet cupcake a goofy name."

"We're only trying to be helpful," Delaney told her, sitting on the couch next to Paige. "Besides, if you and Kev won't decide, someone's got to help out the wee nipper."

"Kev says he picked the girl's name. If it's a boy, it's up to me. It's too much pressure," she complained.

"Then go back for another ultrasound and get the sex," Paige said briskly. "That way you can be prepared."

Delaney rolled her eyes. "Says the woman who will know the sex of her child a week before conception. Hey, ow," she said, rubbing her ribs and eying Paige reproachfully. Paige gave her a sunny smile.

"I think it's kind of nice," Trish put in. "I mean, what else out there in life can be truly a surprise?"

"That's kind, Trish," Kelly said. "At least someone cares about me."

"Well, if you're going to pout, here." Sabrina handed her a glass.

Kelly took it and sniffed. "What's this?"

Sabrina's lips twitched. "A virgin mimosa."

"That's it, you're all uninvited from the wedding."

"Wait a minute, I flew in from Portland for this," Thea protested.

"Come on, I guarantee we'll take you out and get you drunk after you've given birth," Delaney promised.

"Swear?" Kelly demanded.

"Cross my heart. So come on, everyone, a toast."

"To what?"

Delaney thought a minute. "To the best thing that's happened to each of us this summer. You first, then pick the next person," she said to Kelly.

"My bodacious ta-tas," she said, peering down proudly at her now generous cleavage. "This pregnancy thing is great."

"I bet it's Kev's best thing of the summer, too," Sabrina said with a grin.

"You know it. He's talking about keeping me permanently pregnant."

"Wait 'til he sees you in that wedding dress," Sabrina said. "The man's going to think he's died and gone to heaven."

"By the way, I pick you," Kelly added.

"Easy peasy. News that PBS is funding Stef's new doc, which means that I'll get lucky all weekend." She winked. "Trish, darlin', on to you."

"Ty wrapping *The Weight of Water* last week and coming home," Trish said promptly.

"How long's it been?"

"Three months, and I only went to visit him once."

"I bet you had plenty of phone sex," Delaney put in slyly.

"Hey guys, my cousin, remember?" Sabrina interrupted. "Too much information."

Trish grinned. "I'll have mercy on you. Cilla, you're up."

"Getting the word that we're opening a Cilla D. boutique in Cancun next month," she said. "As designer, I'm going to have to be there for the opening. And you're such supportive friends I'm sure you'll all fly out to be there with me, right?"

"You betcha," Delaney said.

"Certainly," Trish agreed.

"Paige is next, by the way."

"Finishing for Alma, the interior designer's Client From Hell," Paige said and downed the rest of her drink. "Can I get a hallelujah on that?"

"Hallelujah," everyone chorused.

"The woman almost drove me out of my mind, but I hung in there."

"What doesn't kill me makes me strong," Thea quoted to her.

"Then I'm entering the Olympic weight lifting competition next summer. Unless I'm somewhere having my head examined," she reflected. "She wouldn't stop with me until I agreed to take on her vacation home."

"Are you nuts?" Delaney demanded.

"I tripled her fee and pushed it out a year and she still wouldn't take no for an answer. Oh, what have I done?" Paige asked, her voice vaguely panicky. "I think I need to start drinking. Oh, and Thea, front and center."

"I got laid," Thea said casually, picking a speck of dust off her sleeve.

Delaney spluttered into her glass. "You *what?*"

Six faces stared at Thea, round-eyed.

"What?" she asked, fighting a grin as she sipped at her mimosa.

"You got laid?" Cilla repeated, as though she'd misunderstood.

"I got *laid*," Thea confirmed. "Not just once. Not even just once a day, as a matter of fact. A *lot* of times a day. 'S like riding a bike." She could feel the goofy smile spread across her face.

"Oh, Thea!" Trish ran over and grabbed her in a hug. "That is so excellent. Good for you!"

"So, is it still going on?" Sabrina asked. "Who is he?"

"A guy up in Portland. Makes beer."

"I like him already," Delaney said.

Paige leaned forward. "Is this serious?"

"A guy up in Portland, remember?"

"So? You'll stay wet." Cilla giggled. "Besides, you could always live down here and just fly in for sex."

"Right now, it's just for fun," Thea said. "I'll let you know if I start signing up for frequent flyer programs."

Delaney raised her glass. "This definitely deserves a toast. To Thea, to all of us."

"For everything we've done, for everything we're going to do," Sabrina put in.

"And for the fact that we've stuck together through it all," Trish added.

Glasses clinked and they drank.

"I swear, though, Thea, if you wind up with this guy long term, I'm never going out of town again," Delaney vowed. "It's dangerous."

"It's not a long-term thing," Thea assured her.

"With this crowd's track record? I'll believe that one when I see it."

BRADY UNLOCKED THE DOOR to Robyn's house and led a panting Darlene inside. "Okay, champ, you've done your workout. Now for the groceries. I'm guessing dinner is a happy time for you, huh?"

Darlene did the swivel thing with her head, pop eyes staring as he slid the lid off the ceramic crock that held the dog food. She bounced around his feet, as much as a dumpling on legs could, anyway. At least until he poured the kibble into the bowl. Instantly, she was all business.

"Yep, all you women are alike. Once I give you what you want, you're done with me."

It was about time to start getting serious about a new dog, he thought as he watched her tuck in. Another border collie. He liked them smart and athletic.

Smart and athletic.

And that quick, Thea was back on his mind. Not that she was ever far from it.

He wasn't used to missing a woman so much. She'd left the day before. Twenty-four hours had passed. No time at all, for most of the relationships he'd had in his life. Forever for this one.

He hadn't liked trying to fall asleep without the warm bundle of her against him. He hadn't liked waking alone. Things came up at the theater that he wanted to talk to her about. Things came up that he wanted to show her. Mostly, he just missed her.

Even with Darlene bouncing around, the house seemed empty. He found himself drifting down the hallway to the room where Thea slept. On the back of the door hung her cream silk robe, with its splashy oriental looking flowers that always gave him vague fantasies of geishas and incense. He brushed his fingers against the fabric to feel its softness. He picked up a sleeve and rubbed it against his cheek.

It smelled like her.

The scent hit him with an almost physical punch and left an ache in its wake, an impossible bone-deep craving to have her there in his arms. If he closed his eyes, he could conjure her in his mind, as vividly as though she were there. Well, not quite. If she were there, she'd have been naked and on the bed. Or on the towel-draped kitchen chair beside it.

He opened his eyes and sighed. She wasn't there and she wasn't going to be for another day and a half.

On a scale of one to ten, it sucked wind.

He wandered over to the chair. He'd had friends before who'd gone off the deep end. How pathetic was it for a guy to be moping like a lovesick fool because his girlfriend wasn't around? Brady had watched them and pitied them, poor slobs.

He'd never in a million years expected to be one of them.

He was Brady McMillan—he didn't do serious. Only serious had happened to him when he wasn't looking, a long, tall drink of serious named Thea Mitchell.

But they had this geographic problem, namely, that she lived in L.A. Soon, he didn't know when, she wouldn't be gone for a day and a half, she'd be gone for good. It wouldn't be one night without her, or two, it would be a whole lot of nights.

His mind balked at the thought. It didn't suck…it was intolerable. Literally. He wasn't prepared to have her gone from his life, not when she was such a part of it, not when she made him complete, not when she made it all work.

Not when he was in love with her.

Good lord.

Three weeks, he thought frantically. There was no way a guy could fall in love in three weeks. There was no way *he* could have fallen in love in three weeks. They barely knew each other. He'd had lots of girlfriends where things had been dandy at the beginning and only went south later. Falling in love this fast made zero sense.

He had a nasty feeling it didn't matter.

If the emotion had been a car, he'd have been walking around it, kicking the tires, opening up the hood. Checking out the driver's seat. Good MPG, definitely fast acceleration.

Time to take it for a test drive, he thought, and really let himself think what it would be like to feel for her that way.

It felt real.

It felt familiar.

It felt right.

Brady had always been a believer that you dealt with what was. Denial was a waste of time. Life was to be experienced, good, bad and…disquieting. He was in love with Thea Mitchell and the smartest thing he could do was accept it.

It wasn't going away.

The second smartest would be to keep this bombshell to himself for a bit. There was stuff going on with Thea that he didn't understand. Smart, strong, gutsy, yeah, but complicated as hell. And until he understood what some of those complications were, he'd be better off slow-playing things. He had a feeling if he mentioned a word of how he felt to Thea, he'd find himself standing and coughing in the middle of the dust cloud she left behind when she bolted.

And there was too much chance of her bolting already.

First things first, get her to realize on her own that they were good together. Of course, then there was the geographic question, which had no easy answer. Maybe she'd move to Portland, he thought hopefully. She loved the city already, he could hear it in her voice. It wouldn't take much to tip it for her.

And if she couldn't see her way clear to doing that, then hell, he'd follow her to L.A.

He wouldn't like it, he recalled Thea telling him.

He'd learn.

Suddenly, he was hit by an overwhelming urge to hear her voice. Not to tell her anything in particular, just to say hello. Lots of people did that, he reasoned, but she was at a wedding, with friends she hadn't seen for a few weeks. She was probably busy hanging out with them.

Didn't matter, he thought as he dialed. She could give him five minutes.

"Hello?"

"Your dog knows more people in this neighborhood than I know in the entire city, and I've lived here my whole life."

Then he heard her laugh and his life fell into place. "Darlene's a natural extrovert."

"She also can't find her way across the front yard without a map."

"Pugs are notorious for lack of direction. That's okay, she's female—if she gets lost, she'll ask. Unlike a guy."

"Feisty."

"I thought that was how you like 'em. So whatcha doing?"

"Walking Darlene, rock climbing. Missing you," he added without thinking and cursed himself. He felt as if he was walking a tightrope in the dark, convinced he was going to make a misstep.

"I miss you, too." Pleasure filled her voice.

"Are you having fun with your buds?"

"Oh yeah. Right now, we're watching a threesome."

"Excuse me?"

She giggled. "A threesome. Randy's getting a blowjob and he's going down on Angel. What?" she said to someone in the background. "Oh, Angela, sorry."

"Wait a minute. Randy? Randy who?"

"Randy the guy who runs the talent agency, and let me tell you, these are some talented women he's got here."

And he could hear the moans. "Where are you?" Brady asked in a strained voice.

"At Cilla's. We're having Kelly's bachelorette party. We've been drinking mimosas all afternoon and now we're onto the porn segment of the festivities."

He let out a silent breath. "A movie."

"Yeah, what did you think?"

"Never mind."

"It's kind of sexy. Seeing her wrap herself all around him makes me wish you were here to wrap around."

"I wish I was there to be wrapped around."

She made a humming noise. "We should watch one together sometime. I bet you'd like it."

"I bet I would."

"Or maybe I can call you later when things are a little more private and we can…entertain ourselves."

And as she purred the words, he felt his cock shift a little. "So ah, you and your friends, are you all bridesmaids or whatever?"

She laughed over the groans of one of the women wailing in ecstasy. Funny how the laugh turned him on ten times as much as the ostensibly sexual noises. Yep. Definitely getting hard.

"I don't think you could find six women less likely to

dress identically and parade in public if you tried. Kelly's sister's standing up with her; we're providing the moral shupport."

His lips twitched. "Moral shupport?"

"Moral support," Thea said with dignity.

"Mimosas all afternoon, I think you said? You must have been trying to drown the pain and sorrow of being away from me."

"Oh, *that's* what I was doing. I wondered. I thought I was having fun with my girlfriends."

"Come home, you can have fun with me," he invited.

She laughed, a peal of delight. "You're cute."

"And you might be just a bit hammered, darlin'."

"Not a chance. I think you're cute when I'm shober."

"Shober?"

"When I haven't been drinkin' mimosas all day, I mean," she corrected.

"I'd start throwing some water in there if I were you or you're going to be hurting tomorrow."

"Oh, mimosas're half orange juice. They're healthy," she informed him.

There was a ringing noise in the background. "What's that?"

"Time for the pizza portion of the festivities," she chirped. "I guess this means I have to go."

"Have fun," he told her and ached to say more.

She laughed at something someone said in the background. "Oops. See—" And with a click, the line went dead.

And he sat staring at the phone, without her.

SHE SHOULD HAVE LISTENED to the advice about the water, Thea thought the next day as she sat between Cilla and

Paige at the wedding. Kelly had gotten them all up at seven. Six hours later, thanks to coffee, water and bagels, Thea was feeling vaguely human.

Kelly, meanwhile, had spent the day chirping about the virtues of being a teetotaler.

"Not only did we have your drinks for you, we're having your hangover for you," Sabrina had groaned. "The least you can do is not rub it in."

The water and coffee had revived them all enough to help Kelly get ready. In honor of the occasion, Thea had even put on lipstick.

And now, the moment was here. Thea hardly recognized Kev up front, with his hair combed for once, his habitual shorts and jeans replaced by a casual suit.

"Did you think Kev even owned a suit?" Paige whispered.

"I would have put odds against it."

"Hey, cut him some slack," protested Paige's boyfriend Zach from the other side of her. "Not all of us are *GQ* ready."

"And that's fine with me," Paige murmured. Zach reached out to put his arm around her shoulders and give her a squeeze. As low key as Kev, Zach had shown up in linen, his charcoal blue shirt buttoned up to the top.

As to Kev, his suit was the only thing about him that was casual—he shifted on the balls of his feet, bounced one fist against his open hand, turned his gaze from point to point. Next to him, Sabrina's husband, Stef, leaned over to offer encouragement.

Or maybe a joke, Thea thought when Kev broke into laughter.

Then the harpist began to play and they all stood and looked back to the head of the aisle, where Kelly had appeared in a gorgeous ivory empire gown.

"Okay, I admit it, I'm a sucker for weddings," Cilla whispered, sniffing. Next to her, her husband, Rand, passed her a packet of Kleenex. And Cilla gave him a bashful, grateful look.

It was being at the wedding, Thea told herself, blinking. Because surely she wouldn't cry at the sight of Cilla's husband handing over a tissue. Except it wasn't the tissue, it was the thoughtfulness, the fact that he'd known to bring one and offered it before she'd asked.

And suddenly Thea understood it, the special glow that surrounded her friends and their men. Not just love, she realized, but connection. Not just passion but comfort, ease. Men who wouldn't just give them hot-eyed looks from across the room but would take time for the small things. Take time to take care.

Thea looked toward the aisle where Kelly was passing, seeing it everywhere along the row. Cilla and Rand, now holding hands. Trish, standing against her live-in lover, Ty, who no longer seemed like a movie star but just like a man who made her girlfriend happy. Sabrina watching her husband, Stef, up at the altar with Kev. Paige and Zach behind her, still unofficial but so clearly a unit that it wasn't hard to see where things would go.

They'd all found it. And as Thea saw Kelly and Kev link hands at the altar, joy seemed to permeate the air, as though the world were somehow golden in this moment. Love. Trish had talked about bottling it. Thea had long wondered if it really existed. But now, watching, she understood that it really was what made everything worthwhile. For the first time in her life, she really believed it.

And as Kelly glowed into wife, Kev grew into husband

and three became one, Thea never noticed the tears that rolled down her cheeks.

SHE STOOD IN BAGGAGE CLAIM a bit after midnight, waiting for her garment bag to appear. This was what you got when you took the final flight out and arrived at the last minute. It had been too hard to leave.

And who knew, maybe her bag hadn't.

Most of the other passengers on her flight were gone, the area was deserted. Thea was starting to seriously wonder if she'd won the lost luggage lottery. One or two hardy souls were still waiting with her, though, so she held out hope.

She sighed, and then recognized her bag as it slid from the top of the ramp to meet her.

"Hallelujah," she muttered and went to reach for it.

"Excuse me, miss, I believe that's my bag," a voice said from behind her. A very familiar voice that she recognized down to the marrow in her bones.

And she turned to see Brady.

She'd have sworn later that there had been some kind of a rent in the space-time continuum, that there was no way she could have seen him and been pressed up against him in the same instant. She didn't remember moving, she didn't remember conscious choice. One minute she was staring at the carousel and the next she had her face buried in his neck, and some part of her relaxed, finally. She could finally breathe. In some indefinable way, things meshed again in her world.

"What are you doing here?" she asked, even as she squeezed him. "It's late. I could have taken the shuttle." It seemed like aeons since she'd held him, aeons since she'd been held. His body against hers was a hard reality.

"I wanted to see you," Brady murmured. "Oh man, you feel so good." He tightened his arms around her.

His lips on hers were both familiar and new. It seemed impossible that she should need to relearn him after such a short absence. And yet, the pleasure was fresh, more vivid, perhaps, after the separation, the longing. He was here.

And that quickly, comfort morphed into heat. Suddenly, holding him, being held wasn't enough. Not nearly. When their mouths met, she could have sworn she felt his sear into her as though he were putting his brand on her, once again. His mouth was hard, impatient, ravaging hers in a way he never had before.

And it was intoxicating.

Without realizing it, Thea found her fingers clenched in his hair as he ran his hands down her, hard and proprietary. Delicious. Exquisite.

And probably not the best idea in the world.

Breaking away from him, she shook her head. "Time to get a grip here."

His eyes gleamed. "Good thinking."

"No. I mean, we're in public."

He snorted. "Who's watching, your bag? There's no one here." As if in agreement with him, the baggage carousel shut down. "Come on, let's go before I decide to take advantage of the quiet."

The walk across to the parking garage seemed to take forever. The minute the elevator doors closed, Brady pressed her back against the wall. In the dim intimacy of the car, she felt only him. And all the stored up heat began to flow.

"Do you know how much it drove me crazy not having you this weekend," he muttered against her skin. His lips were hot with desperation, as though he'd devour her. His hands were on her, squeezing her ass, covering her breasts, tormenting the nipples. And oh, she couldn't get enough air, she was gasping because it was so hot, so arousing, so damned desperate, the way she'd always dreamed of being wanted.

With a ding, the elevator stopped. The doors opened on Brady's soft oath.

"Come on," he muttered, taking long-legged strides into the silent garage, almost dragging her in his urgency. Thea's pulse roared in her ears as they wove their way through the rows of cars until the hood of his Jeep appeared before them. She turned for the passenger side but she didn't get far. Brady spun her around, pressed her back against the hood of the Jeep, fusing his mouth to hers as though she were his source of oxygen.

Lust exploded through her. She could feel the front bumper behind her calves. She could feel how wet she was as he ran his hand up under her skirt, she could feel how hard he was.

"I want you inside me," she whispered.

"Not until you come." And then he was dropping to his knees before her to take her with his mouth, pulling aside the barrier of lace and satin, taking her up so fast she was dizzy with it, until she could only lie back against the still-warm metal of the hood and close her eyes to let the sensation flow through her. And as though the time apart had stored it up, she felt the arousal grow and burn and intensify until it burst through her, leaving her to shudder out her climax.

He was rising, turning her around almost before she'd finished. She felt his warm hands parting her thighs, eager fingers sliding up her skirt and then he was thrusting himself up inside her so hard and so strong that it was all she could do not to cry out.

This, yes, this. It didn't matter if it didn't make her come. Orgasm was irrelevant next to this hard, driving reality, this utter saturation of intensity, this sense of being coupled to some raging force. This sense of being coupled to his pleasure. Thea leaned over the hood and Brady covered her with his body, his arms stretching along hers to clasp her hands, their fingers intertwining.

And to Brady it seemed like forever, it seemed like an instant, it seemed like everything. And it seemed like his world in that moment was perfect and complete and sane as he stroked once, twice, three times to explode in an orgasm that felt like it burst from his very bones.

"Welcome home," he whispered against her neck, and knew that his home was in her.

"WE WERE LUCKY we didn't get arrested," Thea said back at Robyn's. The lamp on the dresser cast a warm, soft glow over the guest room that she'd made her own.

"Sweetheart, it would have been worth it." Brady kicked off his shoes and pulled off his shirt.

"Do you think they caught us on camera?"

He considered. "Probably. I'm betting we made some poor security schlep's night."

"Mmm. You made my night." She flowed up against him. "Thanks for coming to get me."

"My pleasure entirely."

"Or thanks for getting me to come."

He kissed her. "My pleasure entirely."

"Oh, I think it was mine, a little, too."

"So you never told me how the wedding was." Brady flopped down on his side on the bed and watched her undress.

"Oh." The smile spread across Thea's face as she slipped

out of her skirt. "It was great. Kelly looked beautiful and Kev—that's her husband—was ready to just eat her up. They looked so happy." She yawned and tossed her shirt on the laundry basket. "They're going to be great together."

"And they've got a kid on the way?"

"Yeah. I'm going to be an aunt, or maybe a fairy godmother, I'm not sure." She reached back to unfasten her bra and let it slip down her shoulders.

Brady wasn't a poetic type, but there was something about watching her undress that was almost lyrical, some symmetry of form and motion, as though the poetry of dance that she'd studied her entire life stayed with her even now. He watched her in the soft light, the smooth length of her arms, the fragile-seeming wrists, the slight curves that always seemed to feel so lush when he had his hands on them. She was beautiful, though she never seemed to realize it. Most women would have slathered themselves in cosmetics, worked it to its utmost. Thea seemed to be comfortable with who she was.

He loved her.

And he didn't see how he could ever stop.

He sat up as she reached for her robe. "Wait."

"What?" She looked inquiringly back at him.

"Come over here."

Her eyes widened. "So soon?"

He shook his head and patted the sheet. "Sit."

Half amused, half puzzled, Thea obeyed, perching on the edge of the bed before him. Across the room, the mirror on the bureau reflected the two of them side by side. Together.

Brady reached out for the long, woven tail of her hair, curling his hands loosely around it, absorbing the feel.

Thea glanced over her shoulder. "What are you doing?"

"Shh. Look forward." He took the end of her braid and wrapped it around his hand. "You never wear it down, do you? It's always in a ponytail or a clip or braided. Why is that?"

"It's a hassle. It gets in the way."

"You could cut it shorter."

She moved her shoulders. "I did for a while but it didn't feel right. I don't know, I like it long."

He leaned in to press a kiss on the nape of her neck. "I like it long, too."

The skin was so soft here, so tenderly girlish. He touched it with the tip of his tongue and he felt her shiver. Sliding the cloth band off of the bottom of her braid, he slowly began to tease apart the cable of hair, feeling the softness, the spring. "Incredible," he murmured. "There's so much of it."

When she started to speak, he shushed her. Gently, almost reverently, he spread the thick mass of it, draping it so that it looked like a dark cloud around her shoulders in the lamp-glow, watching her in the mirror across the room. Their eyes met in the looking glass. Something shifted within him then, something that had been put in motion when he'd found himself without her, when he'd felt her against him, hell, maybe even the first time he'd laid eyes on her.

"Look how beautiful you are," he whispered, staring. "I can't get enough of you." He pressed his lips to her shoulder. So soft, so smooth, so lovely.

His love.

And Thea felt beautiful, for perhaps the first time ever. She felt gorgeous, she felt treasured.

She felt loved, as though that same golden feeling of the wedding had come with her. And for this time, this precious time, she let herself glory in it.

It was a night for magic and they found it in each other. A gentle breeze of evening cool stirred the sheers at the windows, bringing in the midnight song of crickets. Where they had come together in heat and urgency, they now joined in gentleness. Hard caresses gave way to the soft smoothing of hand over skin. It wasn't about the destination; it was about the journey. They had all the time in the world.

There were moments in life that you knew, even as they were happening, you'd remember forever. When they lay down beside each other, Thea wanted to weep at the pleasure of his naked body against hers. Instead of the flame of passion, theirs was a luminescent warmth, emotion rendered as desire. And somehow the known became fresh, with endless nuances even as they touched one another in all the familiar ways. Hand on breast, body against body. He touched, she shivered. She pressed, he groaned.

And when they found pleasure, it ran through them both as though they were connected. His pleasure matched her own, enhanced her own. His body tightened, but she was the one who trembled. She moaned at the wet slide of his fingers and his were the eyes that darkened almost to black with arousal. Release, when it came, flowed from one of them to the other.

And when they spiraled down into sleep, they did it as one.

13

THE LAST CLASS OF the night was a memory when the telephone rang. Thea sat at Robyn's desk in the studio office, working on the choreography for the theater opening. Making a face, she lifted the receiver. "Rose City Ballroom," she said automatically.

"G'day, Sheila."

"Robyn! How are you? How's 'Strailya?"

"Fabulous," Robyn said dreamily. "Tall and blond with these great smiles and pecs like you wouldn't be—"

"I was asking about the country," Thea said, fighting a smile.

"And I'm giving you the highlights."

Thea set down her pen. "I take it you've been spreading goodwill among the locals?"

"Oh, I'm the goodwill princess. I've got so much goodwill, I make Miss Universe look like a piker."

"No kidding. Boxed any kangaroos yet?"

"No, but I've gone a few rounds with some other lads," Robyn said. "And dived the Great Barrier Reef."

"Ayers Rock?"

"Big," she said. "Red. Had dinner with a redhead the other night, by the way…"

"Wait a minute, are you on the outdoor tour of Australia or the sex tour?"

"I have to pick?" she huffed.

Thea grinned. "I'm glad you're having such a good time."

"Me too, although I can't believe that I have to come home in a week. Where did all the days go?"

"It's all those orgasms. They screw up your time sense."

"I'll say. So how's everything?"

Thea leaned back in Robyn's desk chair and turned it around to look at the lights glimmering outside. "Oh Robyn, it's amazing. I'm dancing and teaching all day and I love it. I'm having the best time."

"You sound happy, hon. Really happy."

"I am. I had no idea how truly wonderful this would be."

"That's great. You know," she said, her voice elaborately casual, "if you wanted to, you could make it permanent. I couldn't offer you full-time work or anything, but…"

The offer was surprisingly tempting. "I live in L.A.," Thea reminded herself as much as Robyn.

"I know. Dumb question. It was just a thought."

"I can stay until you find a new part-time instructor, though. No rush there."

"Oh, you say that now. Wait until the Portland mist starts to fall."

Thea laughed. "You people can't scare me with that."

"So how's the theater project going? Everything okay? You taking care of the McMillans?"

She couldn't prevent the satisfied little chuckle. "Oh, I'm taking care of the McMillans."

There was a pause. "Taking care or *taking care?*" Robyn asked.

"Taking care," Thea said smugly.

"Oh, no," Robyn squealed. "You're sleeping with him." She paused. "Aren't you?"

Thea leaned her head back. "Yes."

"No wonder you sound so happy. Good sex does that for you, and I'm betting the Love God is even better than the Aussies."

"He's rocked *my* world," Thea said.

"So how long?" she demanded.

Thea thought about it. "Week before last," she said, surprised. "Wow. It seems like longer."

"It's all those orgasms," Robyn said dryly. "They screw up your time sense."

"I guess."

"And the theater?"

"I'm working on the choreography for the opening right now. Everything's under control," Thea assured her. "Don't worry."

"I always worry."

"Hey. Vacation, babe? That means no work, no business, no worries. The studio is cool."

"For now."

"Everything's going to be fine."

"Sure. And I'll win the lottery. Or hell, you and Brady'll get serious, and you'll move to Portland and we'll become partners. Perfect."

Perfect, Thea thought. She lived in L.A., she thought again. "Things will work out somehow."

"I know. And I know it's getting late there, so I should let you go. Don't forget, my return flight info is stuck on the refrigerator. You still going to be able to come get me?"

"I wouldn't miss it. Oh, hey, by the way, I am going to have to be gone a couple of days after you come back. My mom's going in for some surgery so I'm going down to be there."

"Nothing bad, I hope."

Outside of having to see her father? "It's a single bypass. They're pretty routine these days."

"You aren't looking forward to it, are you?" asked Robyn, who knew a thing or two about Thea's family.

"About as much as a root canal," she said, keeping her voice light. "She'll be fine. We'll all be fine."

"And then you get to come back and have more sex," Robyn reminded her. "What could be better than that?"

"Hard to think of much."

"Hard being the operative word. Okay, I'm going to let you get going. Oh, and give Brady a kiss for me tonight," she added. "Tell him thanks from me."

"Thanks for what?"

"For making you sound like you do."

Thea hung up the phone, still smiling. Give Brady a kiss? She liked the sound of that. So what if he was probably still finishing up brewing at the Lincoln School? No reason she couldn't stop by and say hello.

No reason at all.

HE LOVED BREWING, Brady thought as he closed the hatch on the brew kettle and went back to cleaning out the mash tun. Yeah, it was a messy job but something about it appealed to the same part of him that as a kid had liked jumping in mud puddles.

And mud puddles never resulted in beer.

He loved the synchronization of it, the experiments, the hundred decisions he had to make each week that controlled whether the result was award winning or slop. Delegate, Michael said, and he'd been working some with an assistant. He couldn't ever see himself totally giving that part of the job up, though.

When he stepped into the microbrewery, he tuned into the process. Brewing kept him focused.

As opposed to focused on Thea.

And the longing hit, as it always did. Didn't matter that he'd seen her that morning. It had been too long, especially when he'd had to do without her during the previous weekend. His bad luck that today was a brew day, which meant he had to wait even longer to see her.

The delegating idea had its points.

Still, at that moment, working hard was probably for the best, he told himself. He needed to take it easy with Thea, with whatever was between them. For his own sanity, he needed to give her space. Give them both space.

So instead of focusing on her, he'd worry about the beer. He hooked up the snakelike tubes to transfer the wort from the brew kettle to the fermenter. After the transfer, he'd pitch the yeast and this particular batch would take care of itself for a few days. This particular batch was also his last for the time being and the process had some wiggle room. He could afford to take a break once the transfer was done, to go outside, get some fresh air. Get away from the pub, even. Not like he'd go see Thea or anything.

Yeah, right.

Grinning at himself, he straightened up from attaching the tubing. And his heart skipped a beat.

Because it was her, standing there at the entry to the brewing area, dark-eyed, a half smile on that gorgeous mouth. No warning, no call. Just her, there, coming to find him.

Coming to find him.

His pulse sped up. It was the first time he hadn't sought

her out. The first time she'd come to him by choice. That had to mean something good, didn't it?

He walked over to her, buoyed by pleasure. "Hey there, tango lady."

"Hey, yourself," she said. And when he reached for her, she went immediately into his arms, drawing him into an openmouthed kiss that had his head spinning. He lingered over her, maybe longer than he should have, but it was hard to stop. Finally, though, he broke away to check on the progress of the wort transfer.

"So what brings you by here?"

"Came to see how the beer's doing. Are you still at it?"

"Just about done."

"What are you making?"

"A dark beer, Oktoberfest."

"In July? I thought Oktoberfest fell in October."

"September, actually, but it's never too early to start Oktoberfest. Any beer that dark needs time to age."

She considered. "Learn new things every day. What about your experiment with the raspberries?"

How could he not love a woman who remembered? "I brewed it last Friday. It'll be ready to try out at the end of next week. If it's good, I might brew up a whole slew of it for the opening of the theater."

"Oh, yeah, speaking of the grand opening, can you get me into the theater at some point to see the stage? Assuming it's done, I mean. I'd like to get a feel for it."

He pulled her to him. "Get a feel for it?" he murmured against her lips.

She paused. "You know what I mean."

"I can only hope. Do you want to go over?"

"Now?"

"Sure. The rewiring's done downstairs. We have lights now, so you can actually see the place."

She glanced at the gleaming copper brew tanks. "Doesn't the beer need you? I'd hate for you to be conflicted."

"Trust me, I'm not conflicted," he assured her. "Tell you what. Once I get the wort moved over, I've got six hours to pitch the yeast. We can do a lot in that time." He leered at her.

Thea slanted a look at him. "Promises, promises."

THE LIGHTS, indeed, were working. And the theater?

When she walked in, it quite simply took her breath away. Under the back wall of the front lobby, they'd uncovered a mural of Hollywood stars. In the auditorium, a dark walnut bar stretched across the back wall. Ahead of her lay a hardwood floored area with brass railings and carved-wood booths. The restaurant, she assumed. The archway over the stage and all the boxes and balconies gleamed with fresh varnish.

Everything was rich, fresh, gorgeous.

"So?" He watched her closely. "What do you think?"

"Oh, Brady." Laughing, she wrapped her arms around his neck. "It's fabulous."

"Really? You like it?"

"I love it. And so will everyone else. I can't believe you've gotten so much done."

"I've only supervised. The crews and the contractor get the credit."

"And if I know you, you've pitched in with them."

He looked embarrassed. "We're on a tight schedule. Anyway, it's not done, yet. Not even close. They're still working on the rooms upstairs and the murals down here. And installing the brewery, fixing up the lobby, putting in the rest of the seats and the furniture." He ticked the items off on his fingers. "We're a long way from done."

"It's gorgeous," she said as they walked down the terraced levels of the restaurant to reach the seating area before the stage. She turned in a full circle, looking all around. "You've done an amazing job with it."

At the stage, he frowned and leaned in to inspect the baseboard at the foot of the front face. "That's not right," he murmured to himself.

"Turning into a perfectionist, are we?"

Pleasure lit his face. "Come up on the stage," he said, seizing her hand to lead her to the stairs. "Sprung, just like you ordered."

Thea stepped out onto the open stage from the wings, feeling that same charge she always did at the space, the possibilities. She could feel the give of the flooring underfoot with each step. Not extreme, but enough to keep it soft. "Oh, this is nice." She took another step, bouncing lightly on her toes. "It's perfect."

"We brought in a special guy to do it."

"You've got to try this out." She held out her arms to him. "Dance with me. Come feel."

"I'll feel you any time." He stepped up to her and pulled her into his arms. He pressed a kiss on her lips. "What about music?"

"I'll hum," she told him.

And they began.

So much had changed, she thought. Less than four weeks before, she'd stood beside him, feeling his hand pressed to her back, thinking it would only be a dance, a touch in passing. Instead, he'd come to mean so much more to her. Instead, he'd become such a big part of her life.

He led her into a basic eight and she pivoted across in front of him, feet soft on the floor. For a novice, he'd learned to give a surprisingly fluid lead into the figures that she'd taught him here and there, when he'd been at the studio, when he'd visited Moonlight and Tango on Fridays.

She'd danced with far more skilled partners, men who'd studied the tango for decades. She never felt a part of them, though, the way she did with Brady. There was the pleasure of the dance, of performing a movement as one half of a whole. Like making love. There was the extra edge of electricity that always flowed between them, the want, the need. And there was the frank physical joy of his touch, of the press of his body, the feel of his hands.

There was something more, though, she realized as they spun around the floor, something else that made dancing with him special.

"What's that song you're humming?" Brady asked.

"An old one. *'Rasgones rojos, corazón rojo.'* Red tears, red heart," she translated.

"More longing?" He swung her into a half-moon. "Let me guess, a woman weeps for her lover…"

"A man," she corrected with a smile.

"A man weeps for his lover, a…sheep named Roja, the prettiest sheep in the flock. But she's toyed with his affections, broken his heart so that all he can do is weep and dance the tango with his sheepdog, Lucky."

"Stop it." She laughed.

"Come on, we've got heartbreak, longing, what else do you want?" He grinned down at her and kissed her on the tip of her nose.

And she felt a sudden wash of pure happiness. It wasn't about heat this time, or arousal or passion. And yet it was.

With Brady, she got both. Beneath the arousal that always thrummed through her when he was around, there was something surprising—comfort. He could make her burn for him, take crazy chances for a moment's enjoyment, and yet she could find other moments like this one, quiet moments, as golden in their own way as the emotions she'd felt at the wedding.

Comfort.

Connection.

Love.

Her foot caught his and she stumbled before righting herself.

"You okay?" Brady asked.

Thea got back in her frame, eyes wide, staring over his shoulder. No, she wasn't okay. What in the world was she thinking? Love? What was between them wasn't supposed to be about love, it was supposed to be about sex, fun, a good time. Nothing more than that. Certainly nothing as serious as love.

Calm down, she ordered herself, flicking up her leg in a *gancho*. It didn't help. It wasn't the wash of intensive carnality that disturbed her but the simple happiness. Why did it threaten her?

Because physicality she could walk away from without a backward glance. Physicality didn't have any hold on her. The way she'd felt with Brady, though, the way she'd *been* feeling with Brady was about a whole lot more than the physical. It was about ties. It meant that he had a lever, that he could control her, the same way the others had.

The same way Derek had.

She was leaving, she reminded herself, almost forcibly putting the anxiety out of her mind. Brady was temporary.

He couldn't have any control over her. Just fun, good times. Everything would be all right.

So why was she shaking?

14

SHE JUST NEEDED TIME to think, Thea told herself as the week passed. If she could get her head on straight, she and Brady could go on like they were before. They were good in bed together, too good to walk away from. They had fun. She was overcomplicating things again, that was all. All she had to do was shove all the love stuff to the back of her mind. It wasn't like she was handing him a lever. Brady didn't try to take over her life, to control her.

Only he did, a voice in her head whispered.

She stiffened, sitting in the driveway outside his house where she'd gone to spend the night. She'd cried off dinner, pleading work, Darlene, her mother's surgery. Somehow, though, when he'd started talking about kitchen chairs and making her laugh, the idea of coming over had become impossible to refuse.

And that was how it always seemed to go.

It wasn't the same, though, she told herself fiercely. Anyway, she'd take the next night for herself, she'd tell him that right up front. All she needed was space and time and she'd be able to hold her line. Time to catch her breath, without his grin, without his touch. Without one of those glances from him that wrapped the two of them together in their own world.

Shaking her head, she reached out for her cell phone.

"Hello?" Her sister answered.

"Lauren?"

"T! How are you?"

Something about Lauren's voice always made her feel steadier. No matter how whacked their parents were, at least the two of them were sane. Mostly. "I'm okay. You?"

"Oh, all right." She didn't sound it, though. There was a flatness to her voice but then she'd probably gotten the same call from their father that Thea had. Discussions with Hoyt tended to do that to a person.

"I take it you got the summons," Thea said.

"Oh yeah. Just about the time I start hoping they've lost my phone number, I pick up and he's there. It's enough to ruin your whole day."

Thea snorted. "Whole day. Try week. How did he get to be such a charmer?"

"Just natural charisma, I guess. No wonder Mom needs heart surgery after living with him her whole life. So are you going down?"

Thea let out a breath. "I guess so. I'd like to show him by staying away, but Mom's the one who's going through the surgery."

"You think this is about her? Don't kid yourself. This is about making Hoyt's life easier, pure and simple."

"I know," Thea said. "I still feel like I should go."

"I know. Me too. That's the truly disgusting part. After all these years, he thinks he can still snap his fingers and have us jump, and we do."

"In this particular situation, it's kind of hard not to. When are you going to get there?"

"I don't know." Lauren sighed. "The surgery's Wednesday, right?"

"Yeah. I'm flying in Tuesday night."

"You still up in Portland?"

"For now," Thea said.

"How's it going?"

"It's good. I like the teaching." A different answer, she reflected, than she'd given Robyn. She hesitated. "I've gotten hooked up with a local guy."

"Meaning for fun or something more?" Lauren asked, a strange note in her voice.

"I don't know." The hot press of anxiety was back. "It started out for fun but it's kind of changing."

"Be careful, T. Last time I saw you, you were in kind of a strange mood."

"I'd turned thirty two days before. Everyone's in a strange mood then. Anyway, how could you tell? You were pretty stressed out over work yourself."

"Yeah." Lauren blew out a breath. "Things are kind of crazy right now. Anyway, just do me a favor and don't dive into anything right away. Give it some time this time around, huh?"

"Trust me, I am. Besides, I've only got another month, month and a half here. It's a built-in safety device." She blinked as she saw the porch light flick on at Brady's. He was expecting her, she reminded herself. "Listen, I've got to get going. As far as Mom's surgery goes, I'm going home Friday morning. If we time it right, we can share a rental car to the airport. Is Tom coming?"

"No."

"Lucky dog," Thea said enviously. "I wish I had an excuse for staying home."

"He's not staying home, T." Lauren's voice got quieter. "We split up."

The words vibrated over the phone. Tom, her sister's husband of four years. Tom, the one who was supposed to wipe the other failures away. Tom, the guy who was supposed to be the one.

And now the ex one.

"But everything seemed fine when I was there," Thea said blankly.

"Did they?" Lauren's voice was quiet.

Not really, now that Thea thought about it. Some subtle tension had invested the house. Lauren had chalked it up to the two of them being busy. Thea had figured it was just the ups and downs of married life. "I'm so sorry, honey," she whispered.

"Me too." Lauren gave a humorless laugh. "I thought the third time was supposed to be the charm."

"Don't blame yourself."

"Who else do I blame?" she returned. "I was the one who walked into the marriage, just like I did all the others. 'This time. This one's going to work. Tom's different.'" Her voice cracked. "The problem is, I'm still the same."

Thea squeezed her eyes closed. Lauren had been her talisman, proof that no matter how bad their childhoods had been, how bad her relationships had been before, things could change. They could get better.

The problem is, I'm still the same.

"Anyway, it's all very amicable. No kids, so there's nothing to fight over," she said aridly.

"Oh, Lauren."

Her sister let out a breath. "It'll be okay. I should be getting used to it by now, shouldn't I?"

"You don't ever get used to it."

"I know. Listen, T, do me a favor. Next time I call you

and tell you I've found the one, will you lock me up some-where until I come to my senses?"

"The right guy for you may still be out there."

"I don't know. I wonder sometimes if maybe I'm just not set up for relationships. Maybe I'm missing something."

And the unspoken words: Maybe we both are.

"That's not true," Thea protested. But when they ended the call, she hung up slowly, staring at the porch light.

HE'D NEVER SEEN so many books. They packed the seven-foot-high shelves that filled the room, lay stacked on tables, even grew up in neat piles against the walls. Behind the counter with the cash registers, they rose to the ceiling, accessed by a rolling ladder. Everywhere as far as Brady could see, there were books, and if there weren't books, there were passageways to more rooms with books. It was like an apartment owned by one of those eccentric packrats who crept around in tunnels carved out of the stacks of magazines and papers and junk.

Thea glanced over at him and shook her head. "You look terrified."

"It's a pretty intense experience."

"I can't believe you've lived here your whole life and you've never been to Powell's. It's an institution," she said, walking through the store's main room. "I thought you Portlanders were supposed to be bookworms. What do you do with yourself all winter while it's raining?"

"I brew beer. Or I go outside and get wet," he added. "I don't melt. Speaking of which, I thought we were hiking."

"Just give me five minutes. I need to pick up a couple of tango and theater books they're holding for me. After that, we can go."

She turned to head down a little staircase that led from the main room into the space beyond.

Brady followed her into the cramped room. "This isn't one of those places where the stairs keep going down and down until you wind up in a dark cellar where the Morlochs live, is it?"

She rolled her eyes at him. "Go back to the main room. They've got windows. And a whole aisle on hiking and outdoors stuff."

"I'd rather do it than read about it."

"Then look up brewing."

"I'd rather do it than read about it."

She kissed him. "Then look up sex and find something new for us to try."

"I'd rather—"

She propped one fist on her hip. "Don't try to tell me you don't read. I've been to your house. I've seen the books."

"True." It wasn't that he didn't read. He'd pick up an outdoor magazine, nonfiction, maybe a mystery or thriller. He usually frequented the small bookstore in his neighborhood, where he didn't have to worry that one of the stacks was going to come tumbling down on him.

"So go browse." She gave him a push and turned away.

Thea had been doing that a lot of late.

Something felt off. He couldn't put his finger on it, couldn't say when things had changed, but something between them wasn't right.

And it was driving him crazy. The thing was, he couldn't exactly ask her a lot about it without sounding paranoid or crowding her. It was probably nothing. She had to be concerned about her mother, even if she did try to pass it off as no big deal. Or refuse to talk about it, if he were honest.

Maybe she was just preoccupied. Maybe she really was just busy. He sure was. The further along they got with things at the theater, the more…idiosyncrasies cropped up. If he wasn't at the theater, he was brewing, if he wasn't there, he was trying to help Michael run the other pubs or watch Michael's kids to give their parents a break.

Was it any wonder their schedules didn't mesh?

Oh yeah, he could come up with all kinds of arguments for how things were probably fine and dandy.

He didn't believe a single one of them.

To take his mind off it, he looked around the bookstore. The problem was, there were too many choices vying for his attention. It was paralyzing. He drifted around a table groaning with those glossy, oversize books people liked to leave out on their coffee tables. *The Complete Fisherman's Guide to Wide-Mouth Bass.* Yeah. There was some excitement. The one on caving was a little more interesting. Cool pictures, but being trapped underground in the dark wasn't really his thing. *Ninety-Nine Bottles of Beer on the Wall.* Now, that was his thing. He was reaching for it when he saw the book behind it.

Runway Confidential screamed the bright pink title in jagged-edged letters. The dust jacket bore a collage of photos of beautiful, stick-thin women prancing around in bizarre-looking clothes. He'd never gotten the anorexic model look—to him, they appeared too weak to even walk across the street. What was sexy about that?

Still, he glanced at it in a sort of repelled fascination. Mannequins, he'd once heard them called and it was true— they looked like those stiff, inhuman figures that stood in store windows. He preferred a woman with a strong, tough body like Thea's. A body that could do things, he thought, his mouth curving at the memory. A body that was down-right extraordinary, with a face to match. A mouth that he couldn't get enough of. Eyes that made him want to dive in so he could see right down into her soul, eyes that were—

Staring up at him from the cover.

He blinked and shook his head. It couldn't be. But he still picked up the book to look closer. And Thea's face, he swore it was her face, looked out at him with pale lips, shadowed eyes. Younger, with inches worth of makeup, but recognizably her. She wore a…dress, maybe, that appeared to be made of paper napkins, her hair twisted up somehow and frizzed.

It had to be a mistake. The table of contents listed stories, not people, so he leafed through the pages, flipping past the drug scandals, the sex scandals, the stories of jail time and nervous breakdowns.

And then he stopped.

Derek's Party Girls, the headline read. This time the picture wasn't from a tabloid. It was real. Taken in a night-club, he thought, the background crowded with a confusion of bodies and neon and brushed metal. She stood amid a cluster of other equally cadaverous women, a scrap of a black mesh miniskirt showing off those mile-long legs, her lips slicked with red, eyes ringed with black.

She hung on the neck of a man who stood in the middle of the group, a man with eyes so pale they looked like ice and about as cold. He had a proprietary hand tucked inside her skimpy wrap shirt and another on her ass. She acted like she didn't notice.

There was more, though, a wrongness about her face, somehow, an unnatural brightness to the eyes, a brittleness, a slack confusion to the mouth.

Thea?

He looked, he saw, he tried to get his head around it.

Coincidence, he told himself, it had to be. They said everyone had a double, maybe this was Thea's. But he knew even as he searched for a caption that he was wrong.

Brady moved his head. He wasn't wrong, this was wrong. This wasn't the person he knew, it wasn't the woman he was in love with.

But it was her. Somehow, impossibly, it was her.

So MAYBE IF she concentrated on the small stuff, it would be all right, Thea thought, mounting the stairs into the main room to see Brady ahead. Like the way seeing him never failed to give her a pulse of excitement. For all the anxiety, there was something about him that made her heart light whenever she saw him. She knew she'd laugh, she knew that whatever happened, she'd have fun. She didn't have to look for warning signs because it didn't matter. It was a temporary gig and she needed to remind herself of that.

For all of his complaining about being in a bookstore, he'd managed to find something to read, she noticed. An endearing seriousness firmed his mouth as he flipped through the book he held. Time to go home, she decided. Forget hiking. Time to go home and jump Brady's bones. Whatever else wasn't working for her right then, that still did.

Quietly, she stole up behind him. "I'm thinking we need to blow this Popsicle stand and go boink our brains out," she murmured in his ear.

When he turned to look at her blankly, her smile slipped. "What's wrong?"

Then she saw the book he held. She saw herself, a person she hardly recognized, a person she'd never wanted to be. A person who'd done things she'd never wanted to do. With Derek, standing behind her.

She dimly heard the book in her hand drop to the floor. "What is that?" she whispered.

He studied her, his eyes unfathomable. "Some supermodel's tell-all book, with 'Derek's Party Girls.' Is this you? I can't find the caption." He glanced from the glossy page to her as though he still couldn't quite believe it.

And she felt sick, as though she were dropping from a great height.

"I mean, it is you, isn't it?" he said slowly, his eyes moving back to the photo. "I knew there was stuff you weren't telling me. I just never figured it was a whole other life."

"Oh, Brady, it's…it was…" It was a past that would never stop haunting her. The parties, the lifestyle, the fast lane turned to nightmare treadmill that she could never escape. Not then and not now, not when it could rise up out of the pages of a book and wrap its cold, relentless fingers around her throat and her life.

Things were only temporary between them, she reminded herself. But somewhere along the line she'd stopped believing that. Somewhere along the line she'd handed him her heart.

As she'd once handed it to Derek.

Hurrying, she headed for the door without a backward glance, unable to breathe.

BRADY SKIDDED OUT onto the sidewalk after her. "Wait." He took a few quick steps. "Hold it, will you wait? What's going on?"

"I want to get out of here," she blurted, something almost hunted in her eyes. "Where's the car?"

"Look, calm down and tell me what's going on."

"I just want to go home," she repeated, her voice high and thin. "Where's the car?"

"Over here. Come on, it'll be okay," he said, moving to put his arm around her, but she flinched away. She'd gone somewhere else in her memories, somewhere far from him, somewhere in those pictures, those parties where the smiles were desperate and the laughter looked too loud.

He was almost bursting on the drive back to Robyn's, wanting to know everything. But he couldn't bring himself to ask. She'd have to tell him.

When he pulled up in front of the house, Thea sat silently for a moment. "It was a long time ago," she said finally, without looking at him. And then she got out of the car without looking back.

Brady jumped out and ran after her. "Hey," he said.

"I'm fine."

"You're not fine."

"I will be." But her hands shook and she couldn't manage to get her keys in the lock. Finally, he took them from her and opened the door.

"Hey, you want space, that's cool. I'm going to take Darlene out for a walk. We can talk when I get back."

"I don't want—"

"It'll be a long walk. Don't worry about it. But leave the door open so I can get in, okay?"

She said nothing, walking into Robyn's place. And he took Darlene out into the quiet afternoon, not paying attention to where he was going, trying to figure out what could have happened to Thea in New York that was so bad she would bury it. And what the wasted person in that photo, wrapped around some guy named Derek, had to do with the woman he loved, the woman who had seemed to shatter in front of him.

The woman he wasn't sure he knew how to piece back together.

Finally Darlene's leash pulled taut and Brady realized that he had walked the pug into exhaustion. "Okay, soldier," he said, scooping her up, "let's go see what Aunt Thea's got cooking for us at home."

The front door was unlocked, he was relieved to find. Inside, he put Darlene down carefully.

"Thea?" he called softly.

The house was silent. He called her name again, more loudly, but there was no response. So he went down the hall. The bathroom mirror was still fogged, from a shower, he assumed. Her bedroom door stood ajar. He gently pushed it open and went in.

On the bed, she lay on her side, wearing her robe, hair still wet. He sat beside her and took up one of her hands. It was ice cold. "Talk to me." His voice broke the hush. "What happened to you?"

"I made over two million dollars is what happened," she said tiredly.

She was serious, he realized. "How?"

"You saw the pictures. How do you think? Modeling."

"Two million?"

"I was very popular."

He shook his head. "What about L.A. and teaching dance? What was all that about?"

She sat up abruptly. "I never said that. You thought what you wanted to."

"What I thought was that there was a whole lot going on with you that you weren't telling me." She had Thea's face, Thea's voice but her gaze was flat, her voice hard. He was in love with her and yet how he wondered if he even knew her at all.

"I'm sorry if I can't be what you want," she said colorlessly.

Then he saw it, the flicker of desperation in her eyes.

"You're what I want." And he was damned if he was going to walk away, no matter how hard she was pushing him. "What happened back there? What happened to you in New York?"

"Nothing."

"Don't kid yourself." Frustration rose in his voice. "It's still with you, whatever it is. I watch you sometimes, you go away in your head and I don't have a clue where."

"What does it matter?"

"Because, dammit, *you* matter."

Her eyes flashed. "What, are you looking for chapter and verse?" She strode out of the room, a movement that looked too much like flight.

Brady followed her. "There's something between us, Thea. Something more than screwing around, and you know it."

She was trapped in the kitchen, a quarry at bay. "What if there is? It's just temporary."

And it was just another attempt to push him away. "Then why are you so scared to talk to me?"

"Fine," she snapped. "You want to know? I'll tell you. I modeled. I did bad things. Bad things happened to me. I made over two million dollars. I left. End of story." She walked out into the living room, sank down on the couch. Out of instinct, he sat beside her. "Oh, what, you're looking for more details?" she asked brightly. "Let's see…I was born. I grew up. Derek found me in a restaurant when I was nineteen."

Derek's Party Girls. "The photographer. The book said he was a hotshot."

"He wanted me for a photo shoot he was doing. Had to have me, and when Derek Edes wants something, Derek Edes gets it." Her smile held no humor. "In this case, he wanted me."

"To go to New York?"

She nodded, still not looking at him. "It seemed like the perfect opportunity—Broadway's where you go if you want to dance and here someone was offering to set me up in New York. I figured I could focus on dance, model on the side." She smiled mockingly, at herself, not him, he realized. "I was more naive than I had any right to be."

"I almost didn't recognize you in those pictures. They made you look like someone else."

"With the right hair and makeup and photographer, anyone can look beautiful."

"I didn't like it," he said flatly. "The way you look now, that's beautiful. Not like that. That was, I don't know, weird and fake."

"Well, the fashion houses liked it. Derek did some fairly innovative stuff with that first spread and it made a name for me. The offers started rolling in. Cover shoots, fashion pages, runway work…" She shook her head helplessly. "There was so much money."

"What about dance?"

"I still took classes. It was the only life I had outside of the fashion industry. I think it was what saved me. That's where I met Robyn." She rose to cross to the window. "He didn't like that I did it, but it was the one thing I held out for."

"He?"

"Derek."

Brady remembered the eyes.

"The day after I got to New York, I was in his studio. The day after that I was in his bed, and the day after that I'd moved in. It was like sliding down a slope of ice."

Barely nineteen, he remembered. And he saw that she was shaking.

"Derek had a rep for making careers—or latching on to the next hot thing. Maybe that's why the other girls were so nasty to me. They wouldn't have been if they'd known what it was like." She stared sightlessly through the glass, at another place, another time. "He controlled everything— what I wore, where I went, what jobs I took, who I talked to. It was like I was some kind of a zombie. I couldn't say no to him. He was, well…overwhelming and I'd been trained pretty well by a father just like him. And he took…everything."

"Your money?"

She made a dismissive noise. "What I made was a pittance compared to Derek. He wasn't after my money, except controlling it. He was after something more…intangible. Anyway, Rita Fletcher, my agent, had gone through a couple of ugly divorces. She insisted that all the money stay in my name. That was the first time he got really angry at me…"

Brady felt the hairs prickle on the back of his neck. "Did he hit you?" he asked carefully.

"No. I wonder sometimes if it might have been easier if he had. Maybe it would have snapped me out of it. I doubt it, though."

"What finally did?"

She gave way and looked at him. "Haven't you heard

enough? Do you have to have every gory detail?" Her voice trembled.

It was here, whatever it was. Whatever had happened, it was this that haunted her. "What was it, Thea?" He stepped up behind her.

"Why do you need to know?"

"I don't need to know but you damned well need to tell someone. You need to get it out of your head before it destroys you. And if we're to have any kind of chance, then yeah, you need to tell me."

"Always a reason, isn't there, Brady? Always an argument, always pushing." She rounded on him. "It's my life."

"It's our life," he countered. "Tell me what happened to you."

"You want to know what happened?" she demanded. "We were at a party. I was talking to a producer I'd met at dance class about choreography. Derek was all smiles and I was so stupid I didn't even realize anything was wrong until we got home. That was when he started ranting. I'd been flirting, he said, making a fool of myself and of him."

She took a shuddering breath. "What I didn't know at the time was that he'd been doing a lot of cocaine and it was making him paranoid. I tried to tell him it was just an opportunity for me to get some dance work. Maybe that was what did it. He went ballistic. And then…" Her mouth opened but for a moment no words came out. "And then he proceeded to show me who was on top in the relationship in the most graphic, fundamental way he could." Her voice was arid, barely audible. "I think you can figure that one out."

If he could have found Derek Edes at that moment, Brady would have wrapped his hands around the man's neck and squeezed the life out of him. He wanted to destroy him, to erase the past, get rid of the shadows in Thea's eyes. But he couldn't. So he did the only thing he could and reached for her.

She flinched. "No. No more."

"No more what?"

"I can't do this. I thought I could but I can't."

"You can't what?"

"Let someone control my life. You, him, anyone."

Brady frowned. "What does that have to do with us? I'm not trying to run your life."

"Oh Brady, you're just like him."

It was the most hurtful thing anyone had ever said to him. "Just like *him?*" he repeated incredulously. "How can you…Thea, I'd never hurt you or try to force you."

She gave him a brittle smile. "Neither did Derek, at first. He just ran my life. Or, excuse me, 'helped me understand what was best for me.'"

"I don't run your life."

"No? Then what are you doing here? I said I was okay."

"You weren't," he said immediately.

"Do you hear yourself? I said I didn't want to talk about it, I *said* I didn't want to tell you about Derek, and you wouldn't stop. You don't listen, you do what you want or you talk me into it. That's how it started with Derek, too."

"Thea," he said desperately, "this isn't us you're talking about. I'm not him. I care about you."

"That's what Derek said."

"I'm not Derek," he bit off. "Can't you understand that? I don't know why we're arguing. I want to be with you, that's the only reason I ever do anything. I love being with you." He swallowed. "I love you."

She fought off the words, threw up her hands. "You

hardly know me. What's it been, a month? You don't love me, you love an idea."

"Don't tell me what I feel."

"Then don't tell me what it is I need. You are like he was. You've got a different style but you're the same. You still never listen. And I'm no better than I was with him. I get around you and I wind up doing what you want, every single time."

The color drained from his face. "I love you," he repeated. "I don't try to make you into someone else. I just want things good for you."

Her laugh ended in a choke. "Oh, I know that line. God, I know it. My father always knew what was best for us, too, until we got away from him. Shoot, he made Derek look like an amateur. So I ran right out and found a boyfriend to get me out of the house, except guess what? He wound up being exactly like dear ol' Dad after a while. Same thing at college, and then Derek. Story of my life. I always say it's going to be different this time and then I look up one day and realize I'm with the same person, only by another name."

Tears began slipping down her cheeks. "I can't do this anymore. I care about you and I'm not going to sit around and watch it fall apart. I'm not going to wake up and find myself in the same sick spot. I'm going to change it this time, no matter what it takes.

"And if that means walking away, then that's what I do."

She stepped closer to him. "Goodbye, Brady." And she pressed her mouth to his.

15

BRADY FLOORED IT from the green light, tires chirping as he turned onto the ramp to I-5. The wind roared in the open windows. He reached over to switch on his CD player, turning it up, then turning it up some more. And then, what the hell, rocketed it up to the top.

Gone. She was gone. His mind shied away from it. Like slipping down a slope of ice, she'd said about Derek. And that was how the past hours had been for him, a slide he had no control over, even as he grasped desperately to avert disaster.

No more of her laughter, no more kisses, no more sharing the golden evenings, no more holding her in the round of the dance.

No more waking with her and knowing that his world was right.

And so he took refuge in anger to escape the tearing, bone-deep, impossible loss. Didn't she understand how wrong she was? How could she throw it away, what they could be together? How could she let the things that bastard had done and said destroy it all? How was it she couldn't believe in them?

How was it she couldn't love him?

He slammed his fist into the wheel.

She hadn't listened to a word he'd said. He might as well not have been talking. All she'd heard were the resonances in her own mind. And he'd been an idiot to sit there arguing with her. He was like Derek Edes? He was like a man who'd hurt a woman, forced himself on her, made her fear?

She wasn't talking to him, she was talking to Edes, she was talking to all those other guys. She was talking to her father, for cripes sake. And holding him, Brady, to account for all of it.

He hit the wheel again. It didn't help.

What he really needed to be doing was climbing the Karate Wall at Smith Rocks or paddling the Rogue. Something that would use up all of him. Something that would extinguish his wanting to howl at the moon to fight off the emptiness.

The problem was, there wasn't any moon and it was full dark on a Sunday night. He'd have gone to one of the pubs and brewed, but the way he felt, if someone even tried saying hello, he'd probably bite their head off.

So he drove, feeling the wind, blasting old Cake and telling himself that it didn't matter, telling himself it wouldn't have worked anyway. Telling himself that she was too damaged to deal with, that he was better off without her.

He only wished he could make himself believe it.

SHE KEPT IT TOGETHER until he left. She listened to the sound of the door closing and she listened to the thundering silence that came after and she fought not to run after him. Instead, she waited for his Jeep to leave.

Only then did she break down.

She'd done the right thing, Thea told herself. For the first time in her life, she'd read the signs, walked away before the debacle. It was hard but she'd done it.

She should have been proud of herself. She should have been relieved.

Why was it she couldn't get her breath?

She thought of the days after she'd fled Derek and New York with Robyn's help, the nightmare of emotional and physical pain, the hunt for sanctuary as though she were some wounded animal going to ground. And the years, the lost years while she waited to heal, never knowing if it was even possible.

With Derek, she'd hurt when she'd made the wrong choice. Now that she was doing the right thing, it hurt even worse. Maybe what Lauren had said was true, that the two of them weren't cut out for relationships. Somewhere along the line, they'd missed some fundamental part of their emotional makeup or it had been distorted.

Maybe they were meant to be alone.

Thea slid down to sit on the floor by the door, shivering. Meant to be alone. For eight years, it had been fine. Now, it sounded like a prison sentence. Darlene ticked up, snuffling, snorting, pushing her nose against Thea, who gathered her into her lap. And as she held onto the tough, warm little body she felt the tightness in her throat ease. She felt herself finally, really let it all go.

And she wept for all that might have been.

HE DIDN'T SLEEP. It wasn't that Brady tossed and turned, he never even bothered to go to bed. Why, when all he'd wind up doing would be staring at the ceiling? Instead, he paced. He did push-ups. He tried to read, but the book only made him think of Powell's and the whole gory scene with Thea. Instead, he grimly waited out the hours.

And watched the brightening sky with disgust.

In the end, he grabbed his mountain bike and hit Forest Park. People ran at dawn. No reason he shouldn't be biking at 5:00 a.m. At least there he was completely present in the moment rather than sliding back into the night before. When you were attacking a fifty-degree incline, you had to be in the moment, unless you wanted to eat a mouthful of bark and pine needles.

He kept at it until his legs and arms were like lead. Then he headed home, which unfortunately gave him time enough to think about Thea. And think he did, from the park to his shower to the theater.

He talked her into things, she'd said. Made her do things she didn't want to. Controlled her. All he wanted to do was go to her, talk to her, try to make her see.

And that was the one thing he couldn't do.

The thoughts were still chasing through his head as he walked through the lobby doors into the Odeon. He wasn't going to let the place remind him of Thea. He wasn't going to think about dancing with her there. He wasn't going to remember holding her in his arms. And he definitely wasn't going to remember how she'd cried out when he'd taken her where she'd never been before.

Just like Edes? Not exactly, babe, Brady thought grimly.

He did his usual circuit, starting with the upstairs, working his way down. Back in the stage wings, the dressing rooms were taking shape as guest rooms, with new walls going up.

Brady stopped at the last room, where the carpenters were busy fitting a new door. He watched them work for a moment.

"Is this the right molding?" he asked, running his fingers over it.

Chad, the older of the two, shrugged. "It's what came with the door. It's prehung."

And that was wrong. "It's not supposed to be," Brady said. "We need to match the other moldings."

"Better ask the boss."

"I think so. Don't do anything on that until I get back," he directed as he walked out.

Ahead, he saw a couple of guys painting the baseboards at the bottom of the front face of the stage. Those were wrong, too. Not the ones he'd signed off on three weeks before with Hal. Then again, there had been a few small changes like that of late. None of them really worth making a big deal over, not in the interest of time. But now…

"Hey, Pete," he said to a passing worker, "where's Hal?"

"With the crew up front working on the bathrooms, last time I saw him."

"Thanks." Brady was already headed to the front of the auditorium as he said it.

The tile of the bathroom in the side hallway sent echoes booming around of fierce debate over the best way to install a wheelchair accessible stall to conform to ADA regulations. Brady knew all the regs by heart because he and Hal had gone through the lot, trying to determine what, exactly, had to be upgraded.

He stuck his head into the room. "Hal, got a minute? I need to talk with you."

Hal glanced up. "Sure. Be right there."

Out in the hall, Brady inspected the candy counter. Hal walked out, wiping his hands on his jeans. "What can I do for you?"

"I was back in the dressing room guest area, where they're putting in the new door."

"Right."

Hal, he noticed, was watching him carefully. "It's a pre-hung door. It doesn't match the other moldings."

"But we—"

"National Historic Landmark, Hal." He let the faintest of edges slip into his voice. "We talked about this. You go with the plan. If you've got to make an exception, you clear it with me." Brady looked at him more closely. "Unless you didn't make the exception," he said slowly. "Did someone else authorize it?"

The silence went on a beat too long.

"Who gave the order?" he asked, though he had a pretty good idea who.

"Well." Hal shifted uncomfortably.

"Who gave the order, Hal?"

"I did," said a voice behind him.

And Brady turned to see Michael. "And I'm not even a little surprised. Morning, big brother."

"'Morning, Brady," Michael said. "You look like hell."

"So do the moldings in the dressing room area. And the stage front baseboards and the replacement doorknobs upstairs. You wouldn't happen to know anything about any of that, would you?"

Michael eyed him for a moment. "Maybe we should take this somewhere else. Excuse us, Hal." Michael headed toward the front lobby.

He was in no mood for it, Brady thought. No mood at all. "You've been doing it right along, Michael, haven't you? You've been doing your little visits, coming in and making changes with Hal behind my back."

"What I've been trying to do is hold this project to budget."

"The project's on budget."

"Exactly. Thanks to me. You didn't leave any room for things to go wrong."

He hadn't spent enough time fighting the trails, Brady thought, not if he could feel this ready to go off again. "You ever notice the slush line item at the bottom of the budget? It's there to cover overages. We don't need all your cute little changes, and those cute little changes might screw up our application to get this place designated a National Historic Landmark."

"It's little stuff."

"It's little stuff that matters. I talked with those people, I found out all the things they look for, including the original damned doorknobs." And suddenly all the anger and frustration coalesced into one point. "Look, did we or did we not agree last month that I'd take over this theater project?"

"Well, we—"

Brady took two steps toward Michael. "Did we or did we not?" He demanded. "You know we did. You said unless I was prepared to do it, it wasn't going to get done. I'm the one who agreed to do it, so fucking well let me do it. You're here every time I turn around, talking to the contractors, giving instructions, countermanding my orders. People don't know who's in charge, you or me."

"Don't you go—"

"So who was the guy who's always been on me about taking a bigger role in the business? Face it, Michael, you're a control freak. You say you want me to do more but you won't let loose. You just want to give me crap and then wade in like the big brother to tell me how it's done."

"That's because you don't know how it's done."

"Yeah, I do," Brady said furiously. "I've been working

my butt off and it's all gone smoothly so far. You always say I never stepped up to do my part but now that I'm trying to, you can't keep your hands out of it."

"And you can't keep your hands off your consultants. Did you sleep with her before or after she started working with us? You are sleeping with her, aren't you?"

Brady fought for calm. "No. I'm not sleeping with her."

Michael studied him. "Ah. I see."

"What do you see?" Brady snapped.

He gave his head a slow shake. "I was out of my mind to ever agree to you running this thing. The minute I did, I knew you were going to screw it up, I just didn't know how. I gotta admit, you've come up with one I never would have guessed. So what's your tango theater going to be without tango, little brother?"

"I'll get a new group in here."

"Why, so you can nail one of them, too?"

The words stung the air. Brady's eyes blazed. "Get off this site," he said, voice low and deadly.

"What do you mean?"

"I mean I want you out of here, for good. You want to come back on this job site, you call me and make an appointment. *Maybe* you'll get in. Until then, you're gone."

"Wait just a goddamned minute. I'm part of this partnership."

"And I'm not taking that kind of talk from anyone, including you. As far as our partnership is concerned, if you don't leave this site right now, I'll have you tossed. Because let's get one thing straight—there's only one person running this project and that's me."

"But I—"

"But you're going, right?" Their eyes locked for a beat.

"I said, 'right?'" Brady repeated. And he stood there long enough to see Michael turn away.

ARRIVALS AND DEPARTURES, Thea thought as she walked through the airport. Coming and going. Going and gone.

Like her and Brady.

Maybe amputees felt this way after the operation, the anesthesia gradually wearing off to unmask a shocking pain and a loss so profound that the mind shied away. And now that the anesthesia of fear and desperation was gone, all she could do was put her head down and endure what followed in the blind hope that one day she would heal. All she was left with was the thought—the hope—that she'd made the right choice.

"Thea!"

Thea glanced over at the escalator to see Robyn waving, tired-eyed but still cheerful. She wore an expedition hat with a leather chin strap and a brand-new golden tan; her backpack was slung over her shoulder.

"G'day, mate," Thea said as Robyn reached for her.

Robyn slung an arm around Thea's shoulders and gave her a squeeze. "I'm excited to see you, trust me. It's just that it's three in the morning by my body clock and I've spent the last twenty hours in a plane. I'm numb."

"Here, let me get that." Thea pulled the backpack off Robyn's shoulder. "Twenty hours?"

"Torture, but worth every minute of it." Robyn gave a jaw-creaking yawn and they walked over to the baggage carousel. "And I had to sit in LAX for almost two hours after I cleared customs. I have a funny feeling that I'm going to last about another hour or two and then completely fall over. Hopefully near a bed."

"Poor baby."

"I know." Robyn pushed out her lip. "How's everything been?"

"All quiet on the western front."

"That's what I like to hear." Robyn started to reach for a bag on the belt but subsided. "Not mine," she pouted. "How about you, everything all right? How's the Love God?" Thea didn't know what expression passed over her face, but Robyn gave her a sharp look. "What's going on?"

"Nothing." Thea tried for offhand. "We're just taking a break." And it was killing her to be standing where Brady had surprised her the night of Kelly's wedding.

"Taking a break? Granted, I only have about two brain cells working, but it's an affair, not a nine-to-five job. What's this break stuff? The last time I talked with you, you guys were crazy about each other. What did he do?"

"Nothing."

Robyn put her hands on Thea's shoulders. "Hey. This is me, remember?"

"I know." Thea sighed. "I just—"

"Hold that thought," Robyn said and grabbed a bag off the carousel. "Okay, start talking," she ordered.

The walking made it easier, but all around Thea, memories of Brady hovered.

"So what happened?" Robyn faced her as they waited at the crosswalk to the parking garage.

Everything and nothing? "Let's say I got a bad feeling of déjà vu."

"What do you mean?"

"When things got bad with Derek, one of the things I realized was that I couldn't put my finger on when it had started. There was never a place to dig my heels in and say no. It was so gradual, the way he took over. He'd give me choices and then take them away. Ask me to pick a restaurant and then argue me into the one he wanted. I'd put on an outfit and he'd talk until he'd changed my mind. He knew what was best, he said, had his finger on the pulse. At first it was little stuff, and always with a laugh." She bit her lip. "Later, it wasn't, any more than it was with my dad."

"And you really think that's what's happening with Brady?" Robyn asked as they stepped into the elevator to the upper levels.

"Yes. No. I don't know," she blurted. They'd kissed here, half devoured each other, she remembered, at the start of one of the most amazing nights she'd ever known. "I say I'm taking a shuttle from the airport, he comes to get me. I say I don't want to go riding, he talks me into it. I say I want the night to myself and the next thing I know, he's there."

"It sounds sweet," Robyn said slowly.

"But that's how it was with Derek at first. And then sweet turned to…" Nightmare. She swallowed. "I've always sworn to myself that I'd never be in that spot again."

The elevator doors opened and they got out and walked to Thea's Prius.

"Do you really think that's what could happen with Brady? Do you really think he's that kind of person?"

Thea's laugh held no humor. "What makes you think I'd know for sure either way? That's always been my problem, I figure out things too late." And she was holding on by a thread, she thought as she unlocked her trunk to put Robyn's bag in. She'd had incredible sex here with him by his car, and then gone home to really make love for the first time in her life. The memories battered at her. "I figure out things too late," she repeated. Her throat tightened. "I'm in love with him, Robyn. And it scares the hell out of me."

"But Thea—"

"I thought I was in love with Derek, and that's what he used against me. With Brady, I don't think I'm in love, I know it." She looked at Robyn, eyes drenched with sorrow. "He could destroy me." And the tears began to fall.

THEA WOKE IN THE DARKNESS, heart thumping. The house was silent, offering no clue as to what had jarred her awake. If it had been a nightmare, she had no memory of it. That was fine with her. Far better to forget than to wake as she had the night before, with the remembered taste of Brady's lips on hers.

The taste she'd walked away from.

Robyn had driven them home from the airport and cancelled evening classes at the studio. Thea would have been useless, she and Robyn both knew, even if she hadn't cried her eyes into puffballs. So she'd given up the distraction. Instead, she'd come home and tried to make the time pass while Robyn slept.

And tried to figure out how to live with the new shape of her life. How did you experience golden hours and then turn around and give it all up? And she could tell herself all she wanted that it hadn't been real, that there'd been darkness waiting beneath. Her heart still ached for it.

She heard a clunk, followed by muffled cursing. At least she didn't have to wonder anymore what had awakened her. Whatever it was, it bore investigating. Thea rose, pulling on her robe and cautiously looked out into the hall.

Darkness, mostly, except for the thread of light at the bottom of the door in the master bedroom. Robyn, of course. Thea padded down the hall. With a forefinger, she pushed the door open. "Robyn?"

Inside the room looked empty except for Darlene, who lay on the bed snoozing. There was an indistinct noise. Then Thea looked to where the closet door stood open, the soles of bare feet poking out at the bottom.

"What are you doing?" Thea asked.

Robyn turned and stuck her head out, swiping a strand of hair out of her eyes. "I'm sorry, did I wake you up? I'm such a dip." She rose and came over to give Thea a hug. "How are you feeling?"

"Like I'll survive, I guess. Thanks for letting me cry on your shoulder."

"Any time."

Thea nodded to the open door. "So what are you doing in there?"

"Cleaning my closet."

"Cleaning your closet? You are aware that it's three in the morning, right?"

"Not for me. For me it's mid-afternoon. Jet lag." Robyn added with a yawn. "I'm sorry. My internal clock went off about an hour ago and I was wide awake. I figured I'd use the time to unpack. Then when I went to put my bag away, some shoeboxes had fallen over and there wasn't any room. So I started going through my shoes and then my clothes and it all just kind of snowballed. Anyway, go back to sleep. I'll be quiet."

Thea shook her head. "I'm awake now. Might as well keep you company."

"Yeah? Cool." Robyn went back into the closet to shove a pile of clothes and shoes out into the room. "I figure I'll take all this to the Salvation Army this weekend."

Thea grabbed a plastic garbage bag Robyn had tossed down and began putting clothes into it. "Not into low cut sweaters any more, I see."

"Too small. They're taking up space."

"You're not one of these people who cleans out your closet every year, are you?" Thea asked suspiciously.

Robyn snorted. "Me? Once a decade, if I'm lucky."

Thea pawed through the pile some more and pulled out a slate blue leather minidress. "Wait a minute, you're out of your mind if you're getting rid of this. Come on, Robyn, you loved this outfit. It was incredibly hot on you."

"That was eight years ago. Besides, I was a teeny bit smaller then."

"Not by much. You still look great."

Robyn rolled her eyes. "Definitely too small."

"How can you get rid of it?" Thea protested. "It would break my heart. I'd starve myself first."

"Sometimes you've got to throw out the stuff that doesn't fit anymore." She flicked a glance at Thea. "Speaking of which, what are you going to do now?"

Thea did a double take. "Man. You don't start with the easy questions, do you?"

"Someone's got to do it."

She bent back to the clothing. "Well, tomorrow I go down for my mom's surgery. Then I come back here and work until you find a new instructor. As soon as you do, I go back home." Away from where memories of Brady stalked her.

"Yeah." Robyn said thoughtfully. "Well, I'll do my best to get someone on board in a hurry, but to be honest I was really hoping you'd like it so much you'd decide to stay."

"I can't, Robyn." Her throat ached. "Everywhere I look, I see him."

Robyn stared at her. "Forget about Brady for a minute. This is about teaching, Thea. You've got a gift for it and you love it. I heard it in your voice last week."

"Of course I love it. I always have."

"So do it. Move up here, work with me. Make a living doing something real." Her eyes flashed with excitement. "I can't pay you big money but I can give you half-time work, pay you at least as much as the nursery did. You can always quit if you don't like it. Come on," she wheedled, "it'll be fun."

"Robyn…" Thea began. It wasn't possible. It just couldn't happen.

"I'll miss you if you go," Robyn barged on. "This is what you're meant to do. As long as I've known you, I've never heard you so happy."

"It wasn't real, Robyn."

"Are you so sure about that?"

At this point, she didn't think she'd ever be sure about anything again.

16

THE AFTERNOON SUN BEAT DOWN on the Blythe pavement with the same paralyzing heat Thea remembered from her growing-up years. The Mitchell house hadn't had air conditioning; probably still didn't. Hoyt had refused to spend the money on it. No need, he'd insisted. Take a shower. Turn on a fan.

The hospital, at least, was cooled. The only problem was making the walk from the parking lot through 110-degree heat to get inside.

"This is it," Lauren told her. "Last chance to change your mind and go get drunk instead."

Hoyt hadn't liked that they were arriving in the afternoon, even though the surgery wasn't scheduled until the following morning. He hadn't liked them coming direct from the airport, or that they were renting a car for the drive rather than depending on him.

There were some things Thea refused to budge on.

"Won't need a sauna for a while," Lauren said wryly as she took a breath of cool air.

Thea smiled at her sister. They shared similar coloring and body types, but Lauren had ruthlessly simple chic that Thea had never achieved, even as a model. All the more surprising to see her drink and curse like a sailor. Then again, their family tended to drive a person to it.

And just about then, that drink was sounding pretty good.

They heard Hoyt's voice before they ever saw him, just as they rounded the corner to the nurse's station on the surgical unit.

"It's a bad location and I want her moved," he demanded.

A pretty young Hispanic nurse faced him. "Sir, it's only for tonight. She'll be taken to the coronary care unit tomorrow after her surgery."

"I don't care what's happening tomorrow." His voice rose as he stood there, tall, rawboned, his face hard and craggy with jutting jaw and narrow eyes.

Before him, the nurse looked like a bunny in front of a bulldozer.

"Will you cover me if I go in?" Thea murmured to Lauren.

"Sure, from a safe distance," she whispered back.

Thea opened her mouth to intercede as a new nurse came up. Or strode up, Thea thought, watching.

"I'm Ruth Huntford, the shift supervisor. Can I help you, sir?"

"Well, I—" Hoyt drew himself up and blinked. In her crepe shoes, Huntford was a match for him in height and more than a match in bulk. He bristled. "My wife's window looks out onto a ventilation tube."

"Your wife is in for pre-op, sir. What's important is that all her testing and prep work takes place on schedule, not that she has a scenic view. We have several more critically ill patients in the other rooms that I'm not prepared to disturb, by moving them—or by loud discussion. I'm sure you understand."

"But—"

"And as Elsa told you, she'll be moved to a room in

CCU after surgery. When we bring her back to the ward, we'll do our best to ensure she has a pleasant view."

"I want her moved—"

Ruth gave him a neutral look. "I'm sure you do, sir. We'll keep that in mind. Good afternoon." And she walked away.

No one walked away from Hoyt like that, but Huntford had managed it. Thea stared at her. "I've never seen anything like that in my life."

"I want her baby," Lauren said.

They waited until Hoyt went down the hall, and followed him to their mother's room. Inside, Betty Mitchell lay in the bed, looking wan.

"Surprise," Lauren said, brandishing the flowers they'd brought.

"Well, look who's finally bothered to arrive," Hoyt said.

It didn't do any good to explain limited flight schedules or work responsibilities. "We're here now," Thea said.

They didn't hug; it was frowned on in her family. Instead, Lauren got busy putting the flowers they'd brought in water and Thea stepped around the bed to take her mother's hand. "How are you feeling?"

"Oh, all right. The angina's not too bad. They say the bypass should fix it."

"She's all right," Hoyt said crossly, sitting down in the room's armchair.

Thea looked at him and her first reaction wasn't—as it had always been before—anxiety, frustration, the dreadful tension of wondering when he'd land the first verbal lash. It was simply this: he looked old.

She hadn't been home in six years. In the intervening time, he'd grown lined, his face and hands spotted by the pitiless desert sun, his white hair thinning. He'd be in his mid-sixties by now, she realized, stooping more, getting smaller.

He adjusted the steel-rimmed glasses he wore. "What are you staring at, young lady?"

"I haven't seen you in a while, that's all."

His eyes narrowed as though he knew exactly what she was thinking. "Look all you want. It'll happen to you too, you know," he said, sounding pleased at the prospect. "Just wait."

"Then I guess I'd better get living my life while I can, hadn't I?" The words popped out before she thought.

"What's that supposed to mean?"

"Lauren and I are staying at the hotel down the street rather than at the house." She hadn't expected to say that, either.

This time, both Hoyt and Lauren stared. "I told you—" he began.

"It's easier for us to be here helping out with Mom, take some of the load off you."

And right now she was going to take the space she needed, dammit, no matter what the price—real or emotional.

BRADY HAD NEVER particularly thought about the fact that he lived alone before. He'd liked it. If he wanted to leave his kayak in the living room while he was working on it, he did. There had been no one to fuss save Spike, who'd kept his comments to himself. Meanwhile, Brady had always been out doing things rather than sitting around. His house might have been empty but he'd never noticed.

Now he noticed. The rooms echoed; if he spoke, his voice sounded too loud. He'd taken to leaving on his eighteen-inch television just to hear voices, although it didn't solve the problem. The sound of a human voice didn't matter a hell of a lot if it wasn't the right voice.

He missed Thea.

It wasn't so bad during the day. He was out, he was busy. The hard part was about nine-thirty at night when he'd catch himself listening for the phone to ring, for a knock at the door. Or he'd wake up at dawn, thinking they should be taking out Darlene, but of course Darlene wasn't any of his affair anymore.

And there was no they.

It was when he caught himself muttering one night in the kitchen that he started to worry. Talking to himself? Not healthy. So he'd decided to get a dog. A border collie would have been his first choice. Which didn't at all explain why he found himself walking through the kennels at the Humane Society.

Why get a purebred, she'd said? Why not rescue a dog? Not that these guys looked much like they needed rescuing, he thought. With the spacious runs and toys and blankets, it was more puppy palace than puppy pound.

"Here's a couple of treats to give out," said the adoption specialist, David somebody or other, handing him dog biscuits. "You said you want a border collie mix?"

Brady didn't bother to look at the I.D. placards on the front of the runs. He was more interested in checking out the dogs. Finding a new buddy meant finding chemistry, the same way you needed chemistry for a friendship.

The same way you needed chemistry for a lover.

Like with him and Thea. He resisted the sudden urge to hit the bars. Dammit, they'd had chemistry, connection, whatever that mystery thing was that made two people golden together. And she'd walked away from it, just walked away. She should have been here with him. They should have been here doing this together.

He stared into the empty run ahead of him. Although it wasn't empty, he realized. It was just that the dog inside didn't rush up to the bars, frenetically jumping, begging for attention. Instead, he sat alert and relaxed in the back corner, not afraid so much as assessing the situation.

"Rocky's new to the shelter," David told him. "He just came in last night so he might be shy."

Brady nodded and crouched down, setting one of the dog biscuits on the floor and putting his knuckles through the tan bars. "Hey, Rock. What's up?"

Rocky tilted his head. He looked like he'd been caught in a spill at the dog equivalent of the paint factory, his fluffy coat a patchy combination of colors. He had a tan muzzle topped by a black bandit mask dotted with gray; two tan spots right over his eyebrows gave him a quizzical look.

He decided Brady looked trustworthy—or at least the dog bone did. Smart dog, Brady figured, feeling the prickle of Rocky's whiskers as the dog sniffed his fingers.

"Do you want us to bring him outside so you guys can get to know one another?" David asked.

"Sure."

It was warm in the concrete-floored outdoor play area. Rocky burst out into it and did a couple of quick laps, thrilled to be out. This time when Brady crouched down, the dog trotted right up. They sat, eye to eye, Rocky tilting his head. The tan eyebrows rose.

"Looking me over, are you?" Brady pulled a ball out of his pocket and tossed it. Rocky dashed madly after it and came trotting back, dropping it in front of Brady, grinning expectantly. So what could he do but throw again, and again?

And after a while, some of the gloom lifted that had been riding Brady's shoulders for days. He rubbed the dog's ears. "Whaddya say, Rock, want to do this? I've got an in with a rawhide bone dealer. Stick with me, buddy, you'll be set."

And Brady would have something that'd make him feel good for a change.

As good as he could.

THE AFTERNOON SUN STREAMED in through the upper-level skylights in the tiny Yuma Airport as Thea and Lauren waited for their flights home. Around them, passengers filed into the terminal.

"You know, I have a whole different feeling about this place on the way home than I did on the way in," Lauren observed, taking a drink of her latte. "It seems so benign now."

"Funny how that works," Thea agreed. "Although it wasn't as bad this time as I'd expected. He wasn't as bad."

"Expect the worst and it's all up from there," Lauren said.

"He's gotten older."

"Not exactly mellowing with age, I don't think."

"In a weird way, I'm not sure I care anymore. So what happens with you and Tom now?"

Lauren's hand tightened on her coffee cup. "I'm not sure. I guess we sell the house. I'll need to get a condo somewhere. Maybe take up tap dancing, who knows." She smiled faintly.

"You think?"

"Or tango."

Or tango. And Thea was back under the trees in the park, feeling Brady holding her, laughing into his eyes. And the longing sliced through her. It couldn't keep happening, she thought rather desperately. It had to start getting easier.

Deep breath, she ordered herself, in and out. She'd made the right choice, the only choice she could have. The phrase had become her mantra. And if she repeated it enough times and stayed calm, everything would be all right.

But the mantra wasn't working so well anymore. "Do you think our lives would have been different if we'd grown up in a different house?" she asked Lauren abruptly.

Her sister looked over at her. "You mean if Dad hadn't been such a miserable sonofabitch, would we have been able to have normal relationships? I don't know. I think about that a lot. I wouldn't have three divorces under my belt, that's for sure."

"Are you positive you're going to have a third one?" Thea asked. "What about giving yourselves some time?"

The gate agent walked briskly into the terminal and closed the boarding door, shutting out the morning heat and the whine of the mini jet engines.

"Possibly," Lauren said. "The problem is what I was talking to you about last week, about being broken somehow."

"Do you really think that's true?"

"I don't know, now. Maybe I've had too much time to think about it the last couple of days, between airports and the hospital. It kind of seems to me, though, that sooner or later you have to stop pointing the finger at other people and start pointing it at yourself."

"Meaning we shouldn't have let Dad get to us?" Thea asked.

"Meaning we should let go of it and live our lives. Just because he gave it to us doesn't mean we have to keep it."

Thea blinked. Robyn, cleaning her closet.

Sometimes you've got to throw the stuff out that doesn't fit anymore.

The words shivered through her. Her father. Derek. All
the old boyfriends. Baggage, the old familiar baggage she'd
carried around far too long. Baggage that had nearly crip-
pled her. Baggage that was destroying her life.

"Do you think it's as easy as that?"

Lauren's eyes softened. "I don't think it's ever easy, T.
But maybe it's worth it. If staying with Tom means I have
to work every day to avoid reacting to something because
of the crap I got from Dad, then maybe that's what I do."

A choice, Thea realized abruptly. She could go on as she
had or she could make a choice, let it go. She could toss
back what she'd learned growing up and say no thanks,
don't want it anymore. Take a chance on Brady.

Take a chance, finally, on herself.

The microphone clicked and the gate agent made a de-
parture announcement for Thea's flight. Portland, Thea
thought. Brady. Home. She looked at Lauren. "I guess I
should start thinking about getting on board."

Lauren gave her a hug. "Maybe we both should."

BRADY STOOD in the cold room, monitoring the gauge on
the big white storage tank as beer flowed through tubes
from the aging tank above. He'd grown accustomed to the
refrigeration over the years and rarely noticed it. He noticed it, though, when the door opened and out of the corner
of his eye he saw Michael walk in.

He didn't say anything. The better part of a week had
gone by and he was still ticked. Maybe it was just the Irish
in him, maybe it was that being hacked off at Michael
gave him one more thing to brood on besides Thea. Not
entirely—nothing was going to do that, not Rocky, not
even a drunken stupor, which he'd tried one night and dis-

counted. Somehow, it wasn't nearly as much fun as it had been at twenty-two, nor was standing in the theater the next morning listening to the pounding of hammers while he waited for his head to roll off his shoulders.

"You used to follow me to Little League." Michael's voice came from behind him.

Brady frowned over his shoulder. "Excuse me?"

"When we were kids. You used to follow me to Little League, down at the school. You were maybe four."

Brady tapped the gauge with his fingernail to free up the needle. "How about that."

"Mom usually stopped you, but you were pretty slippery, even then. I remember one day you got past her. You were tagging after me. I yelled at you to go home and kept on walking. I didn't want to get to practice late and I didn't want to haul my kid brother all over the neighborhood and get crap about it from Freddy Medavoy and his buddies."

"Good old Freddy."

"'Course, it didn't matter. Turned out, they cancelled practice because the coach got sick. Me and Richie Cameron were walking home when we came across Medavoy and his guys pounding on a neighborhood kid."

"That sounds like Freddy," Brady said, "always pounding on someone."

"Yeah, except this time it was you."

Brady gave Michael a quick look. "Medavoy?"

"Yeah."

"He never bugged me."

"Not after that day, he didn't," Michael said with relish. "That day they roughed you up plenty. We showed 'em, though. Richie and I, we came up quiet. Got 'em when they weren't looking and beat the snot out of them. Told Medavoy the next time he went after you, I'd use the baseball bat if I had to."

"Would you have?"

"Never had to find out." He shoved his hands in his pockets. "The thing is, I kind of got used to watching out for you after that. It's a hard habit to break."

"I started being able to beat the snot out of people on my own after a while." Brady kept his voice neutral.

"I know."

"Not to mention give myself a kick in the ass when I need it."

"I'm starting to see that. I'm just saying, it takes time for some of us to catch up."

Brady looked at him steadily. "I know."

Michael blew out a breath. "I screwed up, okay? I was out of line. I agreed to you taking on the theater and I should have left you to it."

For a moment, Brady stood, trying to detect a wobble of the earth on its axis. Michael McMillan wasn't in the habit of admitting he was wrong. "It's not the help and advice I minded. It was the way you handled it. Pushing me into things. Overriding me."

"I know," Michael said. "You're not my kid brother anymore."

"Yeah, I am. It's just that I don't follow you to Little League now. We're always going to be brothers, Michael. But we're partners, too. That's a choice—your choice to treat me as an equal, my choice to step up and be one. And I'm taking it."

"I've noticed. It's going to take me a while to get used to the new and improved Brady."

New? Maybe. Improved?

That had been Thea. She'd been there, backing him in what he wanted to do, making him believe he could. Being with her had made him want to be the best version of who he was, all the time. Being without her? It was taking everything he had to hang in there.

He checked the gauge on the tank. "The new beer's in," he said.

"Oh yeah? What have you got up your sleeve?"

"A raspberry ale. Something new. Maybe we should go upstairs and try it out."

"Maybe we should," Michael said, nodding slowly, "maybe we should."

Upstairs, the lunch crowd was starting to arrive. The raspberry ale was a pale gold with a hint of blush. Brady raised his pint. "So here's to you. I never realized how much work you put into these renovations until the theater. It's been a real eye-opener."

"For both of us."

They tapped glasses and drank. Michael took a swallow, considered, took another. "Raspberry, huh?"

"Yeah. What do you think?"

"Not too hoppy, nice berry overtone, crisp finish." Michael took another sip and grinned. "I think we've got a winner. What are you calling it?"

"El Corazón Rojo."

"El Corazón Rojo?"

"Red Heart. A tango. It's for the opening of the theater."

The bartender stopped before them. "Oh, hey, Brady, I didn't know you were around." She slid beer mats under their glasses. "Someone called for you a while ago."

"I've been down in the cold room. What'd he want?"

"She."

And the hairs rose on the back of his neck. "She?" Michael gave him a sharp look.

"Yeah. She didn't leave a number. Said you would know her. Funny name…Tanya? Tia?"

"Thea?"

"Yeah, Thea."

Okay, so he had sucked down some beer. That didn't explain the sudden rush. "Did she say what she wanted?"

Cassie glanced down the bar to where a customer was flagging her. "Uh, no. I assumed you'd know. Sorry." She hustled away.

She'd come looking for him. It could be about the theater. It could be about the tango lessons.

It could be about them.

And what if it was? Did he really want to hear it or was he walking into more drama? He'd known she had secrets, he'd known she was complicated. But there was such a thing as too complicated.

So why did he still need her?

He looked up to see Michael watching him closely. "Everything okay?"

Brady nodded. "Yeah. You know, I think I'm going to go back downstairs. Got some stuff to do. We cool?"

"We're always cool, dude."

"All right. Give my best to Lindsay and the kids."

"I'll do that."

"And I've got a meeting with Dana Tuesday morning to talk about artwork for the rooms. Stop by if you want."

"I'll let you know if I decide to," Michael said.

"Great." Brady rose and headed toward the stairs to the basement, then stopped and turned back. "Hey, Michael?"

"Yeah?"

"Thanks for the Medavoy thing."

Michael's eyes crinkled. "Any time, bro, any time."

THE DIRECT APPROACH was best, Thea decided as she walked into the Cascade Brewery. Find him, talk to him and hope that he'd give things another try. Give her another try.

Lunch was over. Only a handful of patrons were still hanging around, either late lunchers or diehard beer hounds. Thea walked up to the bar. The wiry blonde behind it looked like she spent a lot of time on the climbing faces. A couple of seats down sat a burly, dark-haired guy with a binder and a beer in front of him; Thea could feel him staring.

The bartender at last made it over to her and tossed down a beer mat. "What can I get for you?"

"Try the raspberry ale," said Binder Guy. "It's a killer."

"Raspberry ale?"

The bartender nodded. "Red Heart. It's brand new. Want to try some?"

Red heart, red tears. "Not right now, thanks. Is Brady McMillan here?"

"I think he's in the basement. Want me to call him up?"

And have the conversation in front of God and everyone? Thea shook her head. "I'll go down there if you tell me where?"

"We don't usually let people—"

"It's okay, Cassie," Binder Guy interrupted. "I'll take her down."

Cassie blinked. "All right. Whatever you say." Thea blinked too, for that matter.

He rose to walk Thea back to the brewing area. "Right over here," he instructed. "I'm Brady's brother Michael, by the way." He stuck out his hand.

"Thea Mitchell."

"Any friend of Brady's…" Michael smiled broadly as they shook.

Any friend of Brady's? That was the question.

Michael opened a door for her. "Go down those stairs and turn left. You'll either find him at his bench or in the cold room."

"Thanks," she said.

He tipped his cap. "My pleasure."

The wooden stairs cut down into the foundation of the building. Thea could feel the air cool as she descended. And she could feel her stomach tighten with nerves. He'd told her he loved her, she reminded herself. Surely there was some feeling left. Surely he'd at least hear her out.

The space was more cellar than basement: stone walls, concrete floor, low ceiling. In the center stood a two-foot-high wooden platform piled with burlap sacks of what she assumed were brewing supplies. A combination work-bench and desk ran along one wall, with record books stacked on a raised shelf. At the back of the area rose the steel walls of what she assumed was the cold room.

Brady was nowhere in evidence.

Thea stood indecisively. Unless Michael was wrong, there was only one place he might be. The cold room. She stepped toward the door as it opened and Brady stepped out. She jumped back, she couldn't help it.

And swallowed. "Hi, can I talk to you?"

Brady just stared. He looked leaner than when she'd seen him last, his hair mussed as though he'd had his hands in it. He wore jeans and a T-shirt that said "I Need a Good Paddling" above the picture of a kayak. He hadn't bothered to shave.

And all she could feel was just stupidly grateful to see

him again, to have a chance to set things straight. Whether he would listen, who knew? With the scene they'd been through after Powell's, she wouldn't have blamed him if he'd decided that she wasn't worth it. All she really had was pure blind hope.

But he nodded, at least he nodded and crossed over to lean against the worktable. "Want a seat?"

"Here's fine." Thea perched on the edge of the wooden platform facing him. That was the easy part.

Now that she was here, she didn't know where to start. She twisted her fingers together. It took clearing her throat twice to speak. "How have you been?"

"Okay. How about you?"

"The same." Thea wet her lips. "Look, Brady, I wanted to talk with you about the other night."

He didn't answer, just looked at her impassively, arms folded loosely over his chest, one ankle crossed over the other.

She took a breath. *Just dive in.* "I said a lot of things. Things I probably shouldn't have. I was pretty upset."

"I noticed."

She raised her chin. "You know about New York. I left there that night, after Derek…finished with me. Robyn helped me get away. I've been on my own ever since and I liked it that way. It was safe. It was comfortable." Her gaze met his. "And then you came along.

"You were supposed to be safe, too. Just for fun, but it turned into way more than that. I wasn't ready and when things heated up with my family and then I saw that book, I…flipped." She looked down at her hands, then up at him again. "But you know that. It was a bad reminder of a really awful time, a feeling I never want to go back to.

"And I said a lot of things that night but I didn't say the one thing I really should have, the important thing. And that's that I love you." Her eyes stung and she blinked furiously. "I wouldn't blame you if you think I'm a head case after all that's happened, but I wanted to tell you. You said you cared for me, that you wanted something more for us. And so I thought—I hoped—that maybe you still might." The words tumbled out. "Because I really want you to be part of my life, some way, some how. So I came here to tell you…"

Why didn't he say something, she wondered desperately. Give her some clue? Was she getting through or was he just enjoying listening to her beg? Because if that was what it took… "Just try," she whispered, "that's all I ask. Just give us a try."

She waited, watched. Nothing. Finally, she moved to rise. "I should go." She had to go because her heart was breaking. She could hear it splinter into separate bits. "I'll see you around."

Brady stirred. "What's changed?"

It was the last thing she'd expected. "What?"

"What's changed?" He dropped his hands down to rest on the bench. "Five days ago, you were telling me that I was the same as that sick bastard in New York. Now you want me in your life. I'm just trying to figure out what's changed here."

It was a wicked jab that took away her breath. But she'd started this thing and she'd finish it. She squared her shoulders. "I shouldn't have said that. It was unfair and I'm sorry," she said, her voice consciously scrubbed of emotion. "I spent a lot of years telling myself that I'd never let it happen again. When I thought I saw it, I overreacted." And yet… "I do think—"

"Yeah." He glanced over at the cold room. "I've been thinking, too. You were wrong but you did have a point—to a point, anyway. I'll cop to it. I get psyched about things and I push. And I'm not always subtle. But it's not all part of some master plot." His gaze came back to hers. "I don't go into it thinking I'm going to bend you to my will or something. I'm not trying to steamroll you. It's just the way I am, no more no less."

His voice was matter of fact, as though he were reciting house rules. Thea frowned. "So what are you telling me, my way or the highway?"

Brady looked at her steadily. "I think that's pretty much a recipe for disaster, don't you? If we're going to try this it can't be anybody's way. It's got to be our way."

She fought down the leap of hope. "Are we going to try this?" she asked.

"Maybe." A smile hovered around the corners of his mouth. "I think it could be worthwhile, don't you?"

And it was like a great bubble of joy began to swell in her chest. "I think you're right."

"So we try it out," Brady said. "I'll try to listen better and you'll try to get to the point that you're not freaked out by my, uh, enthusiasm. Just smack me and tell me to back off if it bugs you. I don't want to always be walking on eggshells."

Her lips twitched. "Sounds good." She stepped over and hooked her fingers in his front belt loops. "Smack you, huh? Can I get that in writing?"

He slipped his hands up to her hips. "Yeah. Me, I just want one thing and one thing only."

"Yeah?" She wiggled against him.

"Besides that." His eyes sobered. "I don't ever want to hear you compare me to that Edes jackass again. I mean it. You have no idea what it was like for me to hear you say that. I love you, Thea. I wanted to kill this guy for what he did to you, and for you to tell me I was like him…" He broke off, his jaw tightening.

Thea framed his face in her hands, staring into his eyes. "I'm sorry," she whispered, kissing his forehead. "I'm sorry." She kissed his cheeks. "I'm sorry." She kissed his eyelids. "I'm sorry." She pressed her mouth to his.

And it was all there, everything they'd felt before and something new, some added depth and intensity that took them to another level. There was promise, there was connection, the leisure to explore, the patience to trust. And underlying it all, the ever-present heat.

Finally, she raised her head and leaned back. "So let me get this straight. Compromise, trust—" she ticked them off "—communication, smacking upside the head—"

"Wild sex," Brady contributed.

"Wild sex. And I'm not ever allowed to compare you to Derek again."

"Right."

"Ever?" She traced a fingertip down his chest. "Not even to say that compared to Derek you're hotter?" She licked his lips. "And bigger?" She caught his earlobe between her teeth. "And a hundred, thousand, million times better lover?" She gasped as he slid a hand up to cup her breast. "And that I could never, ever love anybody as much as I love you?"

Brady pulled her to him. "I suppose I could handle having you compare me that way."

"Then I hope you've got a lot of time because I'm just getting started."

He leaned in and pressed a kiss on her. "Baby, I've got all the time you need."

* * * * *

Don't miss the final outing of the
Sex & The Supper Club with Delaney's story.
Available April 2007 from Harlequin Blaze!

Happily ever after is just the beginning...

Turn the page for a sneak preview of
A HEARTBEAT AWAY
by Eleanor Jones

Harlequin Everlasting—
Every great love has a story to tell. ™
A brand-new series from Harlequin Books

Special? A prickle ran down my neck and my heart started to beat in my ears. Was today really special?

"Tuck in," he ordered.

I turned my attention to the feast that he had spread out on the ground. Thick, home-cooked, ham sandwiches, sausage rolls fresh from the oven and a huge variety of mouthwatering scones and pastries. Hunger pangs took over, and I closed my eyes and bit into soft homemade bread.

When we were finally finished, I lay back against the bluebells with a groan, clutching my stomach.

Daniel laughed. "Your eyes are bigger than your stomach," he told me.

I leaned across to deliver a punch to his arm, but he rolled away, and when my fist met fresh air I collapsed in a fit of giggles before relaxing on my back and staring up into the flawless blue sky. We lay like that for quite a while, Daniel and I, side by side in companionable silence, until he stretched out his hand in an arc that encompassed the whole area.

"Don't you think that this is the most beautiful place in the entire world?"

His voice held a passion that echoed my own feelings, and I rose onto my elbow and picked a buttercup to hide the emotion that clogged my throat.

"Roll over onto your back," I urged, prodding him with my forefinger. He obliged with a broad grin, and I reached across to place the yellow flower beneath his chin.

"Now, let us see if you like butter."

When a yellow light shone on the tanned skin below his jaw, I laughed.

"There…you do."

For an instant our eyes met, and I had the strangest sense that I was drowning in those honey-brown depths. The scent of bluebells engulfed me. A roaring filled my ears, and then, unexpectedly, in one smooth movement Daniel rolled me onto my back and plucked a buttercup of his own.

"And do *you* like butter, Lucy McTavish?" he asked. When he placed the flower against my skin, time stood still.

His long lean body was suspended over mine, pinning me against the grass. Daniel…dear, comfortable, familiar Daniel was suddenly bringing out in me the strangest sensations.

"Do you, Lucy McTavish?" he asked again, his voice low and vibrant.

My eyes flickered toward his, the whisper of a sigh escaped my lips and although a strange lethargy had crept into my limbs, I somehow felt as if all my nerve endings were on fire. He felt it, too—I could see it in his warm brown eyes. And when he lowered his face to mine, it seemed to me the most natural thing in the world.

None of the kisses I had ever experienced could have even begun to prepare me for the feel of Daniel's lips on mine. My entire body floated on a tide of ecstasy that shut out everything but his soft, warm mouth, and I knew that this was what I had been waiting for the whole of my life.

"Oh, Lucy." He pulled away to look into my eyes. "Why haven't we done this before?"

Holding his gaze, I gently touched his cheek, then I curled my fingers through the short thick hair at the base of his skull, overwhelmed by the longing to drown again in the sensations that flooded our bodies. And when his long tanned fingers crept across my tingling skin, I knew I could deny him nothing.

* * * * *

Be sure to look for
A HEARTBEAT AWAY,
available February 27, 2007.

And look, too, for
THE DEPTH OF LOVE
by Margot Early,
the story of a couple who must learn that
love comes in many guises—and in the end
it's the only thing that counts.

HARLEQUIN Romance®

From reader-favorite

MARGARET WAY

Cattle Rancher, Convenient Wife

On sale March 2007.

**"Margaret Way delivers...
vividly written, dramatic stories."**
—*Romantic Times BOOKreviews*

---

*For more wonderful wedding stories,
watch for Patricia Thayer's new miniseries
starting in April 2007.*

Rocky Mountain
BRIDES

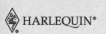

HARLEQUIN®

EVERLASTING LOVE™

Every great love has a story to tell™

Save $1.⁰⁰ off

the purchase of any Harlequin Everlasting Love novel

Coupon valid from January 1, 2007 until April 30, 2007.

Valid at retail outlets in the U.S. only. Limit one coupon per customer.

5 65373 00076 2   (8100) 0 11302

HEUSCPN0407

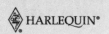 **HARLEQUIN**®

EVERLASTING LOVE™

Every great love has a story to tell™

Save $1.⁰⁰ off

**the purchase of
any Harlequin
Everlasting Love novel**

Coupon valid from January 1, 2007
until April 30, 2007.

Valid at retail outlets in Canada only.
Limit one coupon per customer.

52607370

REQUEST YOUR FREE BOOKS!

2 FREE NOVELS PLUS 2 FREE GIFTS!

HARLEQUIN®

Blaze®

Red-hot reads!

YES! Please send me 2 FREE Harlequin® Blaze® novels and my 2 FREE gifts. After receiving them, if I don't wish to receive any more books, I can return the shipping statement marked "cancel." If I don't cancel, I will receive 6 brand-new novels every month and be billed just $3.99 per book in the U.S., or $4.47 per book in Canada, plus 25¢ shipping and handling per book and applicable taxes, if any*. That's a savings of at least 15% off the cover price! I understand that accepting the 2 free books and gifts places me under no obligation to buy anything. I can always return a shipment and cancel at any time. Even if I never buy another book from Harlequin, the two free books and gifts are mine to keep forever.

151 HDN EF3W   351 HDN EF3X

Name	(PLEASE PRINT)	

Address		Apt.

City	State/Prov.	Zip/Postal Code

Signature (if under 18, a parent or guardian must sign)

Mail to the **Harlequin Reader Service®**:
IN U.S.A.: P.O. Box 1867, Buffalo, NY 14240-1867
IN CANADA: P.O. Box 609, Fort Erie, Ontario L2A 5X3

Not valid to current Harlequin Blaze subscribers.

Want to try two free books from another line?
Call 1-800-873-8635 or visit www.morefreebooks.com.

* Terms and prices subject to change without notice. NY residents add applicable sales tax. Canadian residents will be charged applicable provincial taxes and GST. This offer is limited to one order per household. All orders subject to approval. Credit or debit balances in a customer's account(s) may be offset by any other outstanding balance owed by or to the customer. Please allow 4 to 6 weeks for delivery.

Your Privacy: Harlequin is committed to protecting your privacy. Our Privacy Policy is available online at www.eHarlequin.com or upon request from the Reader Service. From time to time we make our lists of customers available to reputable firms who may have a product or service of interest to you. If you would prefer we not share your name and address, please check here. ☐

HB07

HARLEQUIN®

Blaze™

COMING NEXT MONTH

#309 BEYOND DARING Kathleen O'Reilly
The Red Choo Diaries, Bk. 2
Hot and handsome Jeff Brooks has his hands full "babysitting" his P.R. agency's latest wild-child client, Sheldon Summerville. When she crosses the line, he has no choice but to follow....

#310 A BREATH AWAY Wendy Etherington
The Wrong Bed
Security expert Jade Broussard has one simple rule—never sleep with clients. So why is her latest client, Remy Tremaine, in her bed, sliding his delicious hands all over her? Whatever the reason, she'll toss him out...as soon as she's had enough of those hands!

#311 JUST ONE LOOK Joanne Rock
Night Eyes, Bk. 2
Watching the woman he's supposed to protect take off her clothes is throwing NYPD ballistics expert Warren Vitalis off his game. Instead of focusing on the case at hand, all he can think about is getting Tabitha Everheart's naked self into his bed!

#312 SLOW HAND LUKE Debbi Rawlins
Champion rodeo cowboy Luke McCall claims he's wrongly accused, so he's hiding out. But at a cop's place? Annie Corrigan is one suspicious sergeant, yet has her own secrets. Too bad her wild attraction to her houseguest isn't one of them...

#313 RECKONING Jo Leigh
In Too Deep..., Bk. 3
Delta Force soldier Nate Pratchett is on a mission. He's protecting sexy scientist Tamara Jones while hunting down the bad guys. But sleeping with the vulnerable Tam is distracting him big-time. Especially since he's started battling feelings of love...

#314 TAKE ON ME Sarah Mayberry
Secret Lives of Daytime Divas, Bk. 1
How can Sadie Post be Dylan Anderson's boss when she can't forget the humiliation he caused her on prom night? Worse, her lustful teenage longings for him haven't exactly gone away. There's only one resolution: seduce the man until she's feeling better. *Much* better.

www.eHarlequin.com

HBCNM0207